THE SUICIDE SHOP

Jean Teulé

Jean Teulé lives in the Marais with his companion, the French film actress Miou-Miou. An illustrator, filmmaker and television presenter, he is also the prizewinning author of ten books including one based on the life of Verlaine. In researching that book he discovered that a group of nineteenth-century poets had founded a review called *The Suicide Shop* and this inspired his novel. He has also written biographies of Rimbaud and François Villon.

Sue Dyson

Sue Dyson was a translator and writer. She was perhaps most widely known as bestselling novelist Zoë Barnes.

THE SUICIDE SHOP

GALLIC

THE SUICIDE SHOP

JEAN TEULÉ

Translated by Sue Dyson

GALLIC BOOKS

London

A Gallic Book

First published in France as *Le Magasin des Suicides*
by Éditions Julliard, Paris
Copyright © Éditions Julliard, Paris, 2007

English translation copyright © Sue Dyson 2008
First published in Great Britain in 2008 by
Gallic Books, 12 Eccleston Street, London, SW1W 9LT
This edition 2022

A CIP record for this book is available from the British Library
ISBN 978-1-906040-09-3

Typeset in Fournier by SX Composing DTP, Rayleigh, Essex
Printed in the UK by CPI (CR0 4TD)
2 4 6 8 10 9 7 5 3 1

1

No sunshine ever penetrates this small shop. The only window, to the left of the front door, is obscured by paper cones and piles of cardboard boxes, and a writing slate hangs from the window catch.

Light from the neon strips on the ceiling falls on an old lady who goes up to a baby in a grey perambulator.

'Aah, he's smiling!'

The shopkeeper, a younger woman sitting by the window facing the cash register, where she's doing her accounts, objects. 'My son smiling? No, he's not. He's just making faces. Why on earth would he smile?'

Then she goes back to her adding up while the elderly customer walks round the hooded pram. Her walking stick and fumbling steps give her an awkward appearance. Although her deathly eyes, dark and doleful, are veiled with cataracts she is sure of what she is seeing:

'But he does look as if he's smiling.'

'Well, I'd be amazed if he were; nobody in the Tuvache family has ever smiled!' counters the mother of the newborn baby, leaning over the counter to check.

She raises her head and, craning her bird-like neck, calls out: 'Mishima! Come and look at this!'

A trapdoor in the floor opens like a mouth and, tongue-like, a bald pate pops out.

'What? What's going on?'

Mishima Tuvache emerges from the cellar carrying a sack of cement, which he sets down on the tiled floor while his wife says: 'This customer claims Alan is smiling.'

'What are you talking about, Lucrèce?'

Dusting a little cement powder from his sleeves, he too goes up to the baby, and gives him a long, doubtful look before offering his diagnosis:

'He must have wind. It makes them pull faces like that,' he explains, waving his hands about in front of his face. 'Sometimes people confuse it with smiling, but it's not. It's just pulling faces.'

Then he slips his fingers under the pram's hood and demonstrates to the old woman: 'Look. If I push the corners of his mouth towards his chin, he's not smiling. He looks just as miserable as his brother and sister have looked from the moment they were born.'

The customer says: 'Let go.'

The shopkeeper lets go of his son's mouth. The customer exclaims: 'There! You see, he *is* smiling!'

Mishima Tuvache stands up, sticks out his chest and demands irritably: 'So what was it you wanted, anyway?'

'A rope to hang myself with.'

'Right. Do you have high ceilings at home? You don't know? Here,' he continues, taking down a length of hemp from a shelf, 'take this. Two metres should be enough. It comes with a ready-tied slip-knot. All you have to do is slide your head into the noose . . .'

As she is paying, the woman turns towards the pram. 'It does a heart good to see a child smile.'

'Whatever you say!' Mishima is annoyed. 'Go on, go home. You've got things to be getting on with there now.'

The desperate old lady goes off with the rope coiled round one shoulder, under a lowering sky. The shopkeeper goes back into the shop.

'Phew. Good riddance! She's a pain in the neck, that woman. He's not smiling.'

Madame Tuvache is still standing near the cash register; she can't take her eyes off the child's pram, which is shaking all by itself. The squeaking of the springs mingles with the gurgles and peals of laughter coming from inside the baby carriage. Stock-still, the parents look at each other in horror.

'Shit . . .'

2

'Alan! How many more times do I have to tell you? We do not say "see you soon" to customers when they leave our shop. We say "goodbye", because they won't be coming back, ever. When will you get that into your thick head?'

A furious Lucrèce Tuvache stands in the shop, a sheet of paper concealed behind her back in her clenched hand. It quivers to the rhythm of her anger. Her youngest child is standing in front of her in shorts, gazing up at her in his cheerful, friendly way. Stooping, she reprimands him sternly, taking him to task. 'And, what's more, you can stop chirping' – she imitates him – '"Goo-ood morn-ing!" when people come in. You must say to them in a funereal voice: "Terrible day, Madame," or: "May you find a better world, Monsieur." And please PLEASE stop smiling! Do you want to drive away all our customers? Why do you have this mania for greeting people by rolling your eyes round and wiggling your fingers on either side of your ears? Do you think customers come here to see your smile? It's getting on my nerves. We'll have to get you fitted with a muzzle, or have you operated on!'

Madame Tuvache, five foot four, and in her late forties, is hopping mad. She wears her brown hair fairly short and tucked behind her ears, but the lock on her brow gives her hairstyle a touch of life. As for Alan's blond curls, when his mother shouts at him they seem to take off, as though blown by a fan.

Madame Tuvache brings out the sheet of paper she's been hiding behind her back. 'And what's this drawing you've brought home from nursery school?'

With one hand she holds the drawing out in front of her, tapping it furiously with the index finger of her other hand.

'A path leading to a house with a door and open windows, under a blue sky where a big sun shines! Now come on, why aren't there any clouds or pollution in your landscape? Where are the migratory birds that shit Asian viruses on our heads? Where is the radiation? And the terrorist explosions? It's totally unrealistic. You should come and see what Vincent and Marilyn were drawing at your age!'

Lucrèce bustles past the end of a display unit, where a large number of gleaming golden phials are on display. She passes in front of her elder son, a skinny fifteen-year-old, who is biting his nails and chewing his lips, his head swathed in bandages. Next to him, Marilyn, who's twelve and overweight, is slumped in a listless heap on a stool – with one yawn she could swallow the world – while Mishima pulls down the metal shutter and begins switching off some of the neon lights. Madame Tuvache opens a drawer beneath the cash register and takes out an order book. Inside it are two sheets of paper, which she unfolds.

'Look how gloomy this drawing of Marilyn's is, and this one of Vincent's: bars in front of a brick wall! Now that I like. *There's* a boy who's grasped something about life! He may be a poor anorexic who suffers so many migraines that he thinks his skull's going to explode without the bandages . . . but he's the artist of the family, our Van Gogh!'

She continues, still lauding Vincent as a worthy example: 'He's got suicide in his blood. A real Tuvache, whereas you, Alan . . .'

Vincent comes over, with his thumb in his mouth, and snuggles up to his mother. 'I wish I could go back inside your tummy . . .'

'I know . . .' she replies, caressing his crêpe bandages and continuing to examine little Alan's drawing: 'Who's this long-legged girl you've drawn, bustling about next to the house?'

'That'th Marilyn,' replies the six-year-old child.

At this, the Tuvache girl with the drooping shoulders limply raises her head, her face and red nose almost entirely hidden by her hair, while her mother exclaims in surprise: 'Why have you drawn her so busy and pretty, when you know very well she always says she's useless and ugly?'

'I think she'th beautiful.'

Marilyn claps her hands to her ears, leaps off the stool and runs to the back of the shop screaming as she climbs the stairs leading to the apartment.

'There, now he's made his sister cry!' yells Marilyn's mother, while her father switches off the last of the shop's neon lights.

3

'When she had mourned Antony's death in this way, the queen of Egypt crowned herself with flowers and then commanded her servants to prepare a bath for her . . .'

Madame Tuvache is sitting on her daughter's bed, telling Marilyn the story of Cleopatra's suicide to help her get to sleep.

'After her bath, Cleopatra sat down to eat a sumptuous meal. Then a man arrived from the countryside, carrying a basket for her. When the guards asked him what it contained, he opened it, parted the leaves and showed them that it was full of figs. The guards marvelled at the size and beauty of the fruit, so the man smiled and invited them to take some. Thus reassured, they allowed him to enter with his basket.'

Red-eyed, Marilyn lies on her back and gazes at the ceiling as she listens to her mother's beautiful voice, which continues: 'After her lunch, Cleopatra wrote on a tablet, sealed it and had it sent to Octavius; then she dismissed everyone except one serving-maid, and closed the door.'

Marilyn's eyes begin to close and her breathing becomes more even . . .

'When Octavius broke the seal on the tablet and read Cleopatra's pleas to be buried alongside Antony, he immediately realised what she had done. First he considered going to save her himself, then hurriedly sent some men to find out what had happened . . . Events must have moved quickly, because when they rushed in they caught the guards unawares: they hadn't noticed anything. When they opened the door they found Cleopatra lying dead on a golden bed, dressed in her royal robes. Her servant, Charmian, was arranging the diadem on the queen's head. One of the men said to her angrily: "Beautifully done, Charmian!"

'"It is well done," she replied, "and fitting for a princess descended of so many royal kings." As Cleopatra had ordered, the asp that had arrived with the figs had been hidden underneath the fruit, so that the snake could attack her without her knowing. But when she removed the figs she saw it and said: "So there it is," and bared her arm, offering it up to be bitten.'

Marilyn opened her eyes, as though hypnotised. Her mother stroked her hair while she finished her story.

'Two small, almost invisible pinpricks were found on Cleopatra's arm. Although Octavius was grief-stricken at her death, he admired her noble spirit and had her buried next to Antony with royal pomp and splendour.'

'If *I*'d been there, I'd have made the thnake into pretty thlippers tho Marilyn could go and danth at the Kurt Cobain dithco!' said Alan. The door to his sister's bedroom was half open, and he was standing in the doorway.

Lucrèce swung round brusquely and glowered at her youngest child. 'You – back to bed! Nobody asked your opinion.'

Then, as she stood up, she promised her daughter: 'Tomorrow night I'll tell you how Sappho threw herself off a cliff into the sea and all for a young shepherd's beautiful eyes . . .'

'Mother,' sniffed Marilyn, 'when I'm grown up, can I go and dance with boys at the disco?'

'No, of course not. Don't listen to your little brother. He's talking nonsense. You always say you're a lump – do you really think men would want to dance with you? Come on, settle down for some nightmares. That's more sensible.'

Lucrèce Tuvache, her beautiful face grave, is just joining her husband in their bedroom when the emergency bell rings down below.

'Well, we are on duty at night . . .' sighs Mishima. 'I'll go.'

He goes downstairs in the dark, grumbling: 'Damn, I can't see a thing. One false step and I could break my neck!'

From the top of the stairs, Alan's voice suggests: 'Daddy, inthtead of moaning about the dark, why not turn on the light?'

'Yes, thank you, Mr Know-it-all. When I want your advice . . .'

Nevertheless the father does as his son suggests and, by the glow of the crackling electric bulb on the staircase, he goes into the shop, where he switches on a row of neon lights.

When he comes back upstairs, his wife is propped up with a pillow, a magazine in her hands. 'Who was it?' she asks.

'Dunno. Some desperate bloke with an empty revolver. I found what he needed in the ammunition boxes by the window so that he could blow his brains out. What are you reading?'

'Last year's statistics: one suicide every forty minutes, a hundred and fifty thousand attempts, only twelve thousand deaths. That's incredible.'

'Yes, it is incredible. The number of people who try to top themselves and bungle it . . . Fortunately *we're* here. Turn off the light, darling.'

From the other side of the wall, Alan's voice rings out: 'Thweet dreamth, Mummy. Thweet dreamth, Daddy.'

His parents sigh.

4

'The Suicide Shop. Hello?'

Clad in a blood-red blouse, Madame Tuvache picks up the telephone and asks the caller to hold the line: 'One moment, sir,' and gives change to a woman whose features are distorted by anguish. She leaves, carrying a biodegradable carrier bag that reads THE SUICIDE SHOP on one side, and on the other: HAS YOUR LIFE BEEN A FAILURE? LET'S MAKE YOUR DEATH A SUCCESS! Lucrèce calls after the customer: 'Farewell, Madame,' then picks up the receiver again.

'Hello? Oh, it's you, Monsieur Chang! Of course I remember you: the rope, this morning, wasn't it? You . . . ? You want us . . . ? I can't hear' – the customer must be calling from a mobile – 'to invite us to your funeral? Oh, that *is* kind! But when are you going to do it? Oh, you already have the rope round your neck? Well, today's Tuesday, tomorrow's Wednesday . . . so the funeral will be on Thursday. Hang on, I'll ask my husband . . .'

She calls to the back of the shop, by the fresh produce display: 'Mishima! I've got Monsieur Chang on the line. You know, the concierge from the City of Forgotten Religions housing estate . . . Yes, you do, the one with the Mahomet Tower. He'd like to invite us to his funeral on Thursday. That's not the day when the new sales rep from Don't Give a Damn About Death is supposed to be coming, is it? Ah, that's the following Thursday, so that's all right, then.'

She speaks into the receiver again: 'Hello? Monsieur Chang . . . ? Hello . . . ?' She hangs up as she realises what's happened. 'Ropes may be basic, but they're effective. We ought to think about recommending them more often. With the celebrations coming up . . . Ah, Marilyn, come and see.'

Marilyn Tuvache is now seventeen years old. Indolent and flabby, with long, pendulous breasts, she is ashamed of her cumbersome body. She's squeezed into an over-tight T-shirt, illustrated with a black-edged white rectangle bearing the slogan: LIFE KILLS.

Wielding a feather duster without conviction, she is moving the dust around at the edge of a shelf displaying razorblades for cutting one's veins. Some of them are rusty. A label beside them explains: EVEN IF YOU DON'T MAKE A DEEP ENOUGH CUT, YOU'LL GET TETANUS.

The mother says to her daughter: 'Go to the Tristan and Isolde flower shop and buy a funeral wreath, a small one, mind! Get them to write on the card: *To our customer, Monsieur Chang, from the Suicide Shop*. He will probably have invited quite a few tenants from the Mahomet Tower, and they'll say: "Our concierge managed not to bungle it." It'll be good publicity for us. Go on! You're always asking what you can do. Then you can take the wreath to the new warden at the cemetery.'

'Aw ... I always get the skivvy's jobs; I'm useless around here! Why don't the boys go?'

'Vincent's inventing in his room and Alan's outside, getting intoxicated on the autumn sunshine. He plays with the wind, chats with the clouds. At the age of eleven ... I don't think he's quite right, that one. Now, off you go.'

Marilyn Tuvache eyes up the man her father is talking to at the back of the shop. 'Why don't the good-looking customers look at me? I wish I was attractive ...'

'You really are plain daft, aren't you! Do you think they come here to flirt? Go on, get going.'

'Why can't we kill ourselves, Mum?'

'I've told you a hundred times: because it's impossible. Who'd look after the shop? We, the Tuvaches, have a mission here! Well, when I say "we", obviously I'm excluding Alan. Now be off with you.'

'Well ... OK ... All riiight ...'

'Poor big ...' Madame Tuvache comes out from behind the counter, her heart touched by the sight of her shapeless daughter leaving the shop. 'At her age I was the same: lethargic, always moaning. I felt stupid until the day I met Mishima.'

She runs her finger along a shelf, collecting a little dust. 'And when I did the housework, the corners were always left out ...'

She picks up the feather duster and resumes her daughter's work, moving the razorblades carefully.

At the bottom of the staircase leading to the apartment, next to the fresh produce section, a waistcoated Mishima is giving his sales pitch to a taller, muscular man:

'If you're asking me for something original and virile, I'd say: seppuku, commonly known as hara-kiri – but that's slang. Now, I don't recommend it to everyone, because it's quite an athletic task. But you're a sturdy fellow; you're surely athletic, aren't you? What is your – Forgive me, if you've reached this stage I should have asked – What *was* your profession?'

'Gymnastics teacher at Montherlant High School.'

'There you go, just as I thought!'

'I can't stand my colleagues or my pupils any more.'

'Dealing with kids can be difficult sometimes,' acknowledges Mishima. 'For example, our last child . . .'

'I thought about petrol or napalm.'

'Ah, a nice immolation in the indoor play area, that's not bad either,' agrees the shopkeeper. 'We have everything you need for that, but, frankly, seppuku . . . Anyway, I'm not pushing you to spend money; it's your decision.'

The PE teacher weighs up the two options: 'Immolation, hara-kiri . . .'

'Seppuku,' Monsieur Tuvache corrects him.

'Does it require a lot of equipment?'

'A samurai kimono in your size. I must have an XXL left, and of course the tanto. People make a lot of fuss about it but, look, basically it's a rather short sabre.' Monsieur Tuvache speaks dismissively, removing from the wall a white – and actually rather long – weapon, which he places in the customer's hands. 'I sharpen them myself. Touch the blade. It goes through you like butter.'

The gym teacher contemplates the glinting blade and frowns while Mishima reaches into a cardboard box for a kimono jacket, which he spreads out in front of him.

'My eldest son had the idea of sewing this red

silk cross onto it, to indicate where to aim the sabre, because there have been times when people aim too high, at the sternum, and it won't go in, or too low, so it goes into the belly. And, apart from severing your appendix, that doesn't do anything for you.'

'Is it expensive?' enquires the teacher.

'Three hundred euro-yens, the lot.'

'Oh! Really? Can I pay by –'

'Credit card?' asks the shopkeeper. 'Here? You must be joking – you might as well suggest a loyalty card while you're at it!'

'The thing is it's an investment.'

'Ah, of course, it's more costly than a can of napalm, but, after all, it'll be your last expense . . . Not to mention the fact that seppuku is the aristocracy of suicide. And I'm not saying that just because my parents called me Mishima.'

The customer hesitates.

'I'm afraid I won't be brave enough,' confesses the depressive teacher, feeling the weight of the tanto. 'You don't do a home service, do you?'

'Oh no!' replies Monsieur Tuvache indignantly. 'We're not murderers, you know. You have to understand that's prohibited. We supply what is needed but people do the deed themselves. It's their affair. We are just here to offer a service by selling quality products,' continues the shopkeeper, leading the customer towards the checkout.

And, carefully folding the kimono, which he slips into a carrier bag with the sabre, he justifies himself. 'Too many people do an amateurish job. You know, out of a hundred and fifty thousand people who make the attempt, one hundred and thirty-eight thousand fail. These people often find themselves disabled in wheelchairs, disfigured for life, but with us . . . Our suicides are guaranteed. Death or your money back! Come now, you won't regret this purchase, an athlete like you! Just take a deep breath and go for it! And anyway, as I always say, you only die once, so it ought to be an unforgettable moment.'

Mishima puts the PE teacher's money into the cash register then, as he hands him his change, he adds: 'Wait a minute. I'm going to tell you a trick of the trade . . .'

He takes a good look around him to check that nobody is listening, and explains: 'When you do it in your dining room, kneel on the ground and that way, even if the blade doesn't go in very deep . . . because it's going to sting a little . . . if you're on your knees, you can just fall onto your stomach and that'll push the sabre in up to its hilt. And when you're discovered, your friends will be really impressed! You don't have any friends?

Well, then, it'll impress the medical examiner who'll say: "This fellow didn't pull his punches!"'

'Thank you,' says the customer, overwhelmed at the thought of what he has to do.

'Don't mention it – it's our job. Glad to be of service.'

5

'Lucrèce! Can you come here!'

Madame Tuvache appears, opening a door under the stairs at the back of the shop. She is wearing a gas mask, which covers her face and neck. The circular goggles over her eyes and the bulky filtration cartridge in front of her mouth make her look like an angry fly.

Dressed in a white overall, she takes off her latex surgical gloves and joins her husband, who has called her over to explain the needs of one of their customers.

'The lady would like something feminine.'

'Won-won-won, won-won-won!' buzzes Madame Tuvache's fly face. Then she realises she is still wearing her protective gear, unfastens the head straps and continues, gas mask in hand: 'Ah, something feminine, well, that has to be poison! It's the most feminine thing there is. In fact, I was just preparing some in the scullery.'

She unbuttons her overall too, and places her paraphernalia on the counter, next to the cash register.

'Poison . . . Now, what do I have to offer you?

Would you prefer a contact poison – one touch and you're dead – one you inhale or one you ingest?'

'Er . . .' says the lady, who wasn't expecting this question. 'Which is the best?'

'Contact poison, it's very fast!' explains Lucrèce. 'We have blue eel acid, poison from the golden frog, night star, elven curse, deadly gel, grey horror, fainting oil, catfish poison . . . Not everything is here, though. Certain items are in the fresh produce section,' she says, pointing to a unit exhibiting a large quantity of phials.

'What about the poison you inhale? What's that like?'

'It's quite simple. You unscrew the top and breathe in the contents of the bottle. It could be spider venom, hanged man's breath, yellow cloud, evil-eye toxin, desert breath . . .'

'Oh, I don't know what to choose. You're having to go to a lot of trouble.'

'Not at all,' replies Madame Tuvache understandingly. 'It's perfectly normal to be undecided. If that's not for you, if you prefer something to swallow, we have vertigo honey, which reddens the skin, of course, because you start to sweat blood.'

The customer frowns.

'Briefly, why do you want to end it all?' Lucrèce asks her.

'I've been inconsolable ever since the death of someone I was close to. I think about him all the time. And that's why I've come here to buy something; I can't think of any other way to forget him.'

'I see. Well, I would recommend strychnine. It's extract of nux vomica. As soon as you swallow it, it makes you lose your memory. That way, you'll have no more suffering or regret. Then paralysis develops and you suffocate to death without remembering a thing. That one's spot on for you.'

'Nux vomica . . .' repeats the bereaved lady, rubbing her tired eyes with her palms.

'But, if you prefer to grieve one last time,' ventures Lucrèce, 'you can also make your own poison. Many women like the idea of mulling over their pain as they prepare for death. For example, digitalis: you crush up some foxglove petals in a mortar, which we have in the fresh produce section. You know, they're those clusters of flowers shaped like drooping fingers, the ones that resemble the limp hands of people overcome by grief. When you've obtained a fine powder, mix it with water and boil it. Then let it cool – that will give you time to blow your nose and write a letter explaining what you've done – then filter the solution. Put it on to boil again until the liquid has evaporated. This will produce a white, crystalline salt, which you swallow. The advantage is that it's not expensive: two fifty a bunch! We've also got *Strychnos* branches for extracting curare, black holly berries for theobromine . . .'

Intoxicated by this succession of possibilities, the customer no longer knows what to think. 'What would *you* take?'

'Me? I've no idea,' replies Lucrèce regretfully. And the look in her beautiful, solemn eyes becomes fixed, as if she were gazing far ahead of her. It's as if she's no longer in the shop. 'We're depressed too, and we'd have plenty of reasons to end it all, but we can't sample our own products or the last one of us to try them would have to pull down the steel shutters pretty fast. And then what would our customers do?'

Madame Tuvache seems to come back to earth. 'What I do know is that cyanide dries out the tongue and creates an unpleasant sensation. So, when I prepare it, I add mint leaves to refresh the mouth . . . Those are the extras our business offers. Alternatively, we also have the cocktail of the day! What did I make this morning?'

She goes back to the slate hanging on the window catch. On it is written, in chalk: SANDMAN.

'Oh yes, Sandman! Why didn't I think of it

before? I'm so scatterbrained at the moment. Madame, you couldn't decide between poisons for contact, inhalation or ingestion. Well, this is a mixture of all three: belladonna, deadly gel and desert breath. So, whichever option you should choose at the last moment, whether you swallow the cocktail, touch it or breathe it in, the game will be up!'

'Right, well, I'll take that one,' the customer decides.

'You won't regret it. Oh! I'm so stupid, I was about to say: "You can tell me how you get on with it." It's that child who's driving me mad!' grumbles Lucrèce, pointing her chin at Alan, who's standing in front of the rope display with his feet together and his hands on his head. 'Do you have children, Madame?'

'I did have one, actually . . . One day he came here to buy a bullet for a .22 long rifle.'

'Oh.'

'He saw everything in black. I could never make him happy.'

'Well, we certainly can't say the same about our youngest . . .' laments Madame Tuvache. 'He sees everything in shades of pink – can you imagine? As if there was any reason for such a thing! I don't know how he does it. And yet I can assure you that we brought him up exactly the same way as the other two, who are depressives just as he should be, but *he* only ever notices the bright side of things,' sighs Lucrèce, raising a hand that trembles with indignation. 'We force him to watch the TV news to try and demoralise him, but if a plane carrying two hundred and fifty passengers crashes and there are two hundred and forty-seven fatalities, he only remembers the number of survivors!' She imitates him: '"Oh, Mother, how lovely life is! Three people fell out of the sky and they weren't hurt at all." My husband and I have pretty much given up. I can assure you that there are times when we would gladly take some Sandman if we didn't have to take care of the shop.'

Intrigued, the customer approaches Alan. 'He's in the corner . . . ?'

The said Alan turns his curly blond head towards her. A broad piece of sticking plaster hermetically seals the child's mouth. On the pink plaster, in felt-tip pen, someone has drawn an evil sneer and a tongue sticking out, with the corners of the mouth sloping downwards – making him look like an extremely bad sort.

While wrapping up the phial of Sandman, his mother explains to the lady: 'It was his big brother, Vincent, who drew the grimace. Personally, I wasn't terribly keen for him to draw it with the tongue sticking out, but it's still better than continually hearing him laughing out loud about how wonderful life is.'

The customer examines the sticking plaster. From the shape of the Elastoplast as it sticks to the lips, it is quite clear that underneath the grimacing lines, the child is smiling. Lucrèce hands the carrier bag to the lady. 'He's being punished. At school, he was asked who suicides were, and he answered: "People being sued."'

6

Vincent's emaciated body is swamped in a grey djellaba patterned with drawings of explosives: sticks of dynamite and black ball-shaped bombs with fuses spitting out yellow and green flashes of light. He is twenty years old. The walls of his bedroom are entirely devoid of decoration. As he sits facing a narrow bed, elbows propped on an overloaded table backed up against a wall, a tube of glue trembles in his hand. The Tuvaches' elder son has striking bushy eyebrows and sports a short, spiky red beard. His breathing is laboured and quivering, and his fixed sidelong look reflects the tragedy of his inner torment. Crêpe bandages compress the entire upper part of his head; he still suffers from violent migraines. Brown crusts swell his thick lower lip, the result of frequently being bitten hard enough to draw blood, while his upper lip is very red and delicate. In the middle it lifts into two points, like the scarlet canopy of a tiny circus tent. In front of him on the table lies a strange, macabre model under construction, while behind him, on the other side of the dividing wall, can be heard:

'*Da-da, doobi-doobi da-da-da!*'

'Mother!'

'What now?' demands his mother from the kitchen.

'Alan's playing happy songs!'

'Oh no, give me strength ... You know, I'd rather have given birth to an entire nest of vipers than bring up that ridiculous child!' grumbles Lucrèce, coming into the corridor and opening the door of her younger son's bedroom. 'Will you give it a rest? How many times have I told you we don't want you to listen to those stupid cheerful ditties? Were funeral marches composed for dogs? You know how much it upsets your brother, having to listen to those cheery songs, and how much it makes his head hurt.' She leaves the room and enters Vincent's, where she's confronted by the debris of the exploded model. 'Oh, well done, you've really done it now!' she says, still talking to Alan. 'Look at this catastrophe your music's caused. You've really done yourself proud this time!'

It's not long before the father of the family arrives. 'What's happening?'

Then Marilyn appears, dragging her feet. All three of them – Lucrèce, Marilyn and Mishima – are here now, surrounding Vincent.

'What has happened,' yells Madame Tuvache,

'is that *your* younger son has been up to his usual tricks again!'

'He's not *my* son,' retorts her husband. '*My* son is Vincent. He's a real Tuvache.'

'And what about me?' asks Marilyn. 'Where's my place in all this?'

Mishima strokes his elder son's bandaged cranium. 'So, what happened? You broke your model?'

'A model of what?' enquires the Tuvaches' daughter.

Vincent sobs. 'The model of a suicide theme park.'

'Of *what*?'

7

'It would . . . It would be like a big fair for people who'd had enough of life. At the shooting gallery customers would still pay, but to be the target.'

As he listens to Vincent, Mishima sits down on the bed.

'My son is a genius.'

'It would be the most deadly amusement park. On the walkways, among the smells of frying chips and the poisonous mushrooms we would sell, tears would trickle softly down the customers' cheeks.'

'Death caps!' cries Mishima, and Lucrèce and Marilyn get carried away too, breathing in the smell of the chips . . .

'Barrel organs would grind out sad songs. Ejection carousels would propel people like catapults, right over the town. There would be a very high palisade from which lovers could throw themselves, just like they'd throw themselves off a cliff, hand in hand.'

Marilyn joins her own hands and rubs them together.

'In the din of the ghost train's wheels, laughter

punctuated with sobs would spin off into an imitation gothic castle full of comical traps, all of them deadly: electrocution, drowning, sharpened portcullises that would slam down into people's backs. The friends or relatives who had accompanied a despondent person would leave with a small box containing the desperate person's ashes, because at the end of the fairground attraction there would be a crematorium, into which the bodies freefall one after the other.'

'The lad is amazing,' says Mishima.

'Father would feed the furnace. Mother could sell tickets . . .'

'And what about me – how would I be of use? Where would I fit in?'

Vincent Tuvache pivots his head so that he almost faces his sister. Oh, the piercing power of his gaze, the ravaged radiance of his anguished eyes beneath his head bandages! Outside in the darkness, through the panes of his sombre room's small window, a neon advertising sign suddenly dazzles him with a crazy intense yellow light. Then the shadows of his face become a very pale green and his short, now pink, beard seems painted by brushstrokes arranged in a star formation. Overexposed in the artificial brightness, he is also haloed by the vibrations of an incredible self-destructive passion. The three people around him are moved by the sound of his heart-rending cry. The light changes and becomes red. It is as if Vincent, who lowers his head, had been caught in the blast from a bomb:

'It would be like when I'm dreaming and I wake up, then I go back to sleep but I'm still forever dreaming of the same fairy tale, the same setting . . .'

'Have you had this project in mind for a long time?' asks his mother.

'On the walkways, employees disguised as evil witches will offer poisoned toffee apples – "Come, Mademoiselle. Eat this poisoned apple . . ." – then they'll go off and see someone else.'

'Actually, I could do that,' suggests Marilyn. 'I'm ugly.'

The elder son sets out all his plans: the cabins on the Big Wheel – the floors of which would give way at twenty-eight metres above ground – and the incomplete Figure of Eight rollercoaster with ascending rails that, after a dizzying descent, would suddenly stop in full flight. He explains the model, which he demolished moments ago with a blow from his fist, while his little brother leaves his room, and passes Vincent's open door humming and snapping his fingers in time:

'*Don't worry, be happy . . . !*'

His appalled mother, curses at the ready,

turns round and clenches her fists at him. To her and her husband, Alan's castanet fingers are an aberration.

8

'In fact, to be honest, Monsieur, we didn't actually want a third child. He was born because we tested a condom with a hole in it: you know, the ones we sell to people who want to die of a sexually transmitted disease.' Lucrèce shakes her head in dejection at this blow from fate. 'You must admit it was pretty bad luck – the *one* time we tried out one of our own products.'

'Well, condoms from Don't Give A Damn About Death are guaranteed porous. You should have trusted us without testing them,' answers the sales representative.

'All the same . . .' sighs Alan's mother as the boy himself suddenly appears in the shop.

'Hell-ooo, Mother! Hell-ooo, Father! Hell-ooo, Monsieur . . .?' he continues, coming over and spontaneously kissing the representative on both cheeks. 'Have you theen? It'th raining. That'th good. We need water, don't we!'

'How was school?' his mother asks him.

'Very good. In the music lethon, I thang and made the whole clath laugh.'

'You see, what did I tell you?' exclaims

Madame Tuvache, meaningfully to the rep.

'It's true that he doesn't seem the easiest of lads . . .' acknowledges the representative, wiping his cheeks. 'I take it the other two aren't like that, though?'

'No, they would have gone past sighing and pushing you out of the way without apologising. Although the elder son has no appetite, he gives us complete satisfaction, almost always shut away in his bedroom as he is, but poor Marilyn, who's almost eighteen, feels oafish and useless here. She's always hot and sweaty. She's searching for her place in life.'

'Hm, mm . . .' mutters the new Don't Give A Damn About Death representative, opening his briefcase and taking out an order book. He looks around him, examining the shop from top to bottom. 'A very fine shop you have here. And it comes as a surprise, all alone as it is, surrounded by tower blocks. Oh yes, the prettiest shop really on Boulevard Bérégovoy! And then there's the outside; your facade is most curious. Why is there a narrow tower on the roof, like a bell tower or a minaret? What was this place before? A church, a chapel?'

'Or a mosque, a temple perhaps. Nobody knows any more,' replies Lucrèce. 'The rooms along the upstairs corridor could have been monks' cells, which were later turned into bedrooms, a dining room and a kitchen. And then the little door on the left-hand landing leads to the worn stones of the tower's spiral staircase, but we never go there. Down at the back, in what must have been a sacristy, I make my in-house poisons.'

The sales rep raps his knuckles on a wall that sounds hollow.

'Did you have everything covered with plasterboard?' Then he examines the displays, commenting on them to himself: 'Double unit in the middle, a simple unit against both of the two lateral walls ... Old-style Delft tiles, good mortuary lighting on the ceiling, an air of cleanliness and on top of that, good heavens, there's a choice ... The slip-knots are here ...'

'By the way, we'll take some hemp from you,' declares Mishima, who's been silent up to now. 'Of an evening, I like twisting the ropes myself while I watch dramas on TV. And, besides, people appreciate handcrafted work. One year, we took some machine-made ropes. A lot of people just ended up falling off their stools.'

'How much shall I put you down for – a bale?' The representative makes a note.

'And some cyanide too,' says Lucrèce, standing in front of the display unit by the left-hand wall, where the phials stand in rows. 'I've hardly got any left. And some arsenic: a fifty-kilogram bag.'

'Put us down for one kimono, size XXL,' adds Mishima.

The representative walks further into the shop, writing down the orders, and arrives at the fresh produce shelves, which astonish him.

'I say, it's oddly empty here: a few digitalis petals, black holly berries, some splendid *Cortinarius rubellus* mushrooms, *Galerina marginata*, but not many creatures in boxes with holes for them to breathe through . . .'

'Ah yes, we've always had a problem with wildlife,' admits Mishima, 'whether it's with golden frogs, trigonocephalus vipers or black widow spiders . . . You see,' he explains to the representative, 'the problem is that people are so lonely that they become attached to the poisonous creatures we sell them. And, curiously, the creatures sense this and don't bite them. One time, do you remember, Lucrèce . . .? A lady customer who had bought a killer trapdoor spider came back into the shop. Now, I was very surprised and she asked me if I sold needles. I thought they were for her to put her own eyes out. Well, not at all: they were to knit little bootees in pearlised cotton for her spider, which she'd named Denise. They had become friends and, what's more, the lady had her at liberty in her bag. She took her out and let her run over her hand. I said: "Put it away!" And she laughed and said: "Denise has given me back my taste for life."'

'Another time,' cuts in Lucrèce, 'a depressive bought a venomous spitting cobra that never spat at him and which the customer ended up calling Charles Trenet. Couldn't he have called it Adolf? We carefully gave our children the names of famous suicides: Vincent for Van Gogh, Marilyn for Monroe . . .'

'And why Alan?' asks the representative.

'If he'd called his snake Nino Ferrer,' goes on Lucrèce, still following her train of thought, 'that we could have understood too.'

'Oh no, really, creatures are disappointing,' intervenes Mishima. 'When the golden frogs escape, they hop all over the shop. And it's really complicated trying to catch them with a net, especially when you mustn't touch them or you're dead. We won't be taking any more wildlife and I don't know what we're going to do with the fresh produce section.'

Sitting on the steps of the staircase that leads up to the apartment, young Alan is holding a small plastic stick topped by a ring, into which he is blowing. Soap bubbles are flying up from it. They rise and fall, float, coloured and shining, in the Suicide Shop. They find their way, carelessly, between the shelving. Mishima's neck sways and bends as he follows their journey.

One large bubble of soapy water happens to burst on the representative's eyelashes. He wipes his eye and, grimacing, heads for his briefcase on the counter: 'I may perhaps have an idea here for your child who's in difficulty.'

'Which one? Alan?'

'Oh no, not him . . . for the girl. At Don't Give A Damn About Death, we've just launched a new product that would hold no dangers for her.'

'No dangers for her?' repeats Lucrèce.

9

'The first of November ... Happy birthday, Marilyn!'

Her mother emerges from the kitchen carrying a metal tray, on which lies a birthday cake in the shape of a coffin. Her father, who is standing beside the round table in the dining room, pops the cork of a bottle of champagne and addresses his daughter as he pours her a glass:

'Hey, that's one year less you have to live!'

The bubbles climb up the glass. Marilyn Tuvache places her index finger on the edge and the bubbles subside. The cake holds mournful sway at the centre of the table, among the remains of the family dinner and in front of Vincent's untouched, empty plate. Mishima tries to serve him some champagne too.

'No thank you, Father. I'm not thirsty.'

His father pours a few drops into Alan's glass. 'Go on! Take it, you ever-happy soul ... to celebrate the coming of age of your sister, who's finished with childhood and adolescence. It's a start.'

The sides of the cake, covered in milk

chocolate, are in imitation of the varnished poplar wood of a coffin. But the dark cocoa-coloured lid, decorated with mouldings, looks like mahogany. About two-thirds down its length, it is open revealing a pillow of Chantilly cream, on which rests a head made from pink marzipan. Curls of lemon peel represent bright blonde hair.

'Oh look, it's me!' exclaims Marilyn, her hands rushing to her lips. 'How beautiful it is, Mother!'

'I didn't have much to do with it,' admits her mother modestly. 'Vincent had the idea and drew it for me. The poor thing couldn't cook it, because of the disgust he feels for food, but he made the candles too.'

The candles, which are beige and twisted like ropes, have been slightly melted in order to twist them into the shape of two standing numbers which burn side by side: one and eight, eighteen. Marilyn picks up the one and moves it to the other side of the eight: 'I'd rather be eighty-one . . .' Then she blows them out as if she were snuffing out her existence.

Mishima claps his hands. 'And now, the presents!'

Marilyn's mother closes the kitchen refrigerator, and returns with a small package that looks like a wrapped barley sugar sweet.

'Marilyn, please forgive the presentation. We

asked Alan to buy some white wrapping paper edged with black, like bereavement cards, and he came back with coloured paper covered in laughing clowns. But you know what your brother's like … It's for you, you're grown up now – from your parents.'

Marilyn, moved by all the attention, peels away the folds of paper at either end of the present and opens it.

'A syringe? But what's that inside, the stuff that looks like water?'

'A terrible poison.'

'Oh, Mother, Father! At last you have given me death. Is it true, I can kill myself?'

'No, not yourself!' exclaims Lucrèce, rolling her eyes to the heavens. 'But everyone you kiss.'

'How?'

'At Don't Give A Damn About Death, they suggested this liquid that they have perfected. You inject it intravenously and you don't get sick; nothing happens to you at all. But in your saliva you develop a poison that will kill everyone who kisses you. Every one of your kisses will be deadly …'

'And as you were trying to find your place in the shop,' went on Mishima, 'well, your mother and I decided that we could entrust you with the fresh produce section. You would be there to kiss those customers who were recommended this type of voluntary death: the *baiser de la mort*, the Kiss of Death . . . !'

Marilyn, who has been sitting limply, gets to her feet, trembling with emotion. 'But,' her father makes clear, 'you must just be careful never to kiss us.'

'Mother, how is it possible to be poisonous without poisoning oneself?'

'Think about creatures – how do they do it?' replies Lucrèce, the specialist. 'Snakes and spiders live healthily with death in their mouths. Well, it will be the same with you.'

Mishima ties a tourniquet above his daughter's elbow. She taps the body of the syringe, forces a drop from the needle's tip and injects the vein herself as Alan watches her. She has tears in her eyes.

'It's the champagne!' she says defensively.

'Right, and what about you boys?' demands Mishima. 'Where are the presents for your sister?'

Vincent, painfully thin and his head bandaged as ever, brings out a voluminous parcel from under the table. Marilyn unwraps the present, the paper decorated with clowns, and her big brother explains the strange object:

'It's an integral motorbike helmet in indestructible carbon fibre – I've reinforced the visor.

Inside, I've fixed two sticks of dynamite from which two strings hang . . . That way, if one day Mother and Father allow us to destroy ourselves, you put on the helmet, fasten the strap under your chin and then you pull on the two strings. Your head will explode inside the helmet without staining the walls.'

'It's a delicate touch, thinking of details like that!' applauds Lucrèce, whose elder son also draws admiration from Mishima: 'Apparently, my grandfather was like that: inventive. And what about you, Alan? What's your present?'

The eleven-year-old boy unfolds a large square of white silk. Marilyn seizes it immediately, rolls it up and tightens it round her neck.

'Oh, a cord to hang myself!'

'Oh no . . .' smiles Alan, showing her. 'It has to be loose, and pretty. It has to be like a caressing cloud around your neck, your shoulders, your chest.'

'What have you bought her?' asks his mother anxiously as she cuts a piece of the coffin-shaped cake and offers it to Vincent.

'No thank you, Mother.'

'I bought it with my pocket money,' replies Alan.

'You must have saved up for a year!'

'Yes.'

Lucrèce stands there with the cake-slice poised in the air above the cake.

'I don't see the point of it,' she continues, cutting another slice of cake.

'It really is a waste of money,' agrees Mishima.

Gazing round at her family, Marilyn floats the scarf gently round her throat.

'I won't kiss you, of course, but my heart wants to.'

10

Night has fallen. In her room, Marilyn has undressed and, standing naked, she plays with the large square of white silk before her reflection in the panes of her window, which looks out onto the City of Forgotten Religions estate. People fall from the balconies of the Moses, Jesus, Zeus and Osiris towers like autumn drizzle.

Monsieur and Madame Tuvache's daughter makes the scarf fly around her. As the silk brushes her shoulders it provokes shivers that arch her back. She lets the pure fabric slide down her buttocks, catches it in front between her legs and throws it into the air above her. There, the white square spreads out like the gracious movement of a principal dancer. It floats down like a slow parachute onto her upturned face. Eyes closed, she breathes out and the silk floats up again. Marilyn catches a corner of it, which she winds around her belly, her hips, like the arm of a man holding her by the waist. Aaah . . . the swish of the scarf rising further between her thighs and catching in her hairs. Aaah . . . Marilyn, ordinarily stooped with drooping shoulders, straightens up.

Aaah ... She arches more when Alan's gift, gathering momentum, rises up her chest and brushes her breasts of which, wrongly, she is ashamed. Their nipples harden, becoming erect. Her breasts are large and magnificent and, with fingers joined behind the nape of her neck, Marilyn is astonished to discover herself like this, reflected in her bedroom window, as the scarf falls back down. She catches it as it reaches her shapely calves, and bends forward. Her backside is splendid, broad beneath a waist that is only the tiniest bit fat. And the silk travels again, revealing to the mixed-up girl the unsuspected harmony of her body. She is the most beautiful girl in the whole district! Not a single girl in the City of Forgotten Religions estate can hold a candle to her. Her little brother's gift, better than a dream ... And the scarf continues its hypnotic, sensual dance across her quivering skin. Marilyn's eyelids lower in an expression of ecstasy unknown to her. But what else is she discovering? Is she becoming Monroe? She parts her lips, revealing a thin strand of ... deadly ... saliva.

11

OPEN OWING TO BEREAVEMENT. The little sign, turned towards the outside and fixed to the front door with a sucker, moves as something above it tinkles. Hanging high on the frame like a little bell, a minuscule skeleton made of iron tubes picks out the mournful notes of a requiem. Then Lucrèce turns her head and spots a young customer entering.

'Hm, you're not very old, are you? How old? Twelve, thirteen?'

'Fifteen!' lies the adolescent. 'I would like some poisoned sweets, please, Madame.'

'Well, listen to you, with your "sweets" in the plural! You can only take one of our fatal delicacies. We couldn't have you distributing them to all your classmates. We're not here to decimate Montherlant High School or Gérard de Nerval College!' says Lucrèce, unscrewing the large lid of a spherical glass jar filled with sweets. 'It's the same with bullets for revolvers – we only sell them singly. A man who shoots a bullet into his head doesn't need a second one! If he demands an entire box, it's because he has something else in mind. And we are not here to supply murderers. Go on, choose . . . but choose well, eh, because in this jar, only one sweet in two is deadly. The law demands that we give children a chance.'

The very young girl hesitates over the chewing gums, paper-wrapped fortune sweets and deadly caramels – half clamshells filled with hard yellow, green or red confectionery, to be licked for a long time because they cause a slow death. By the window, there are large paper cornets: lucky bags, blue for boys and pink for girls. She doesn't know what to choose, but finally seizes a fortune sweet.

Young Alan is sitting beside his mother, drawing large suns on pages from an exercise book. 'Why do you want to die?' he asks.

'Because life isn't worth the trouble of living,' replies the girl, who is around the same age as the Tuvaches' youngest child.

'That's what I half kill myself trying to tell him!' cuts in Lucrèce, filled with admiration for her young customer. 'Here, take a leaf out of her book,' she continues, addressing her son.

The schoolgirl approaches Alan, and confides: 'I'm alone against everyone, misunderstood in a cruel world, and my mother is such an idiot . . . She confiscated my mobile, all because I went over the time allocation by a few hours. I mean, what's the use of a telephone if you can't call people with it? I'm sick of it. If I had an allocation of fifty hours, I wouldn't have exceeded it . . . In fact, she's jealous because she doesn't have anyone to call, so she takes it out on me: "Blah, blah, blah! Why do you spend hours calling Nadège? You could just go and see her, she only lives opposite." So I don't have the right to stay in my room, is that it?' demands the girl indignantly. 'Why should I go out? I don't want to see the sun, that crummy star. It's good for nothing, the sun . . .' she continues, looking at Alan's drawings. 'It's too hot and nobody could live there.'

She turns back to the cash register and pays for her fortune sweet. 'My mother doesn't realise how much time I have to spend getting dressed, doing my hair and putting on my make-up before I go out. I wasn't going to spend all that time in front of the mirror when I could just pick up the phone!'

Tinkle, tinkle – the mournful notes of a requiem – and the girl leaves the shop, unwrapping her sweet (the only possible response to her drama). The youngest Tuvache child leaps off the stool, runs after her and, on the doorstep, he snatches the sweet from her and then throws his hand to his mouth. Lucrèce leaps out from behind the counter, yelling: 'Alan!'

But it was a joke. The child gets rid of the possibly deadly sweet by throwing it in the gutter while pale-faced Madame Tuvache holds him tightly in her arms: 'You'll be the death of me!'

Alan smiles, one cheek against his mother's chest. 'I can hear your heart beating, Mother.'

'Fine, but what about me, and my sweet?'

The distraught girl is so disgusted with life that Lucrèce goes back into the shop to fetch the sweets, and returns to offer her another chance to choose from the glass jar.

The schoolgirl seizes a fortune sweet, and swallows it immediately.

'So,' the owner of the Suicide Shop asks her, 'is your mouth becoming dry? Can you feel the burning as the arsenic trickles down your throat?'

'Nothing but sugar . . .' replies the girl.

'Well, it really isn't your day,' Lucrèce is forced to acknowledge. 'Come back another time.'

'Unless you change your mind,' Alan continues.

'Of course, unless you change your mind,' his mother repeats mechanically, still emotional. 'But . . . what on earth am I saying?'

Inside the shop, she gives her son a shove. He laughs, and accuses her: 'It's you as well; you make me say silly things too!'

12

'Often people ask us why we named our youngest "Alan". It's because of Alan Turing.'

'Who?' asks a surprised fat woman whose crestfallen features seem deeply shadowed.

'Don't you know Alan Turing?' asks Lucrèce. 'He was an Englishman whose homosexuality got him into trouble with the law and who's regarded as the inventor of the first computer. During the Second World War, his contribution to the final victory was of great importance, for he succeeded in deciphering the Enigma system: the electro-magnetic coding machine that enabled the German high command to transmit messages to its submarines. Without Enigma the messages were indecipherable by the Allied secret services.'

'Oh, right, I didn't know . . .'

'He's one of History's great forgotten figures.'

The hesitant customer gazes around the shop with eyes made weary by the doleful regret she feels for her faded dreams . . .

'I'm telling you about this,' Lucrèce goes on, 'because I saw you just now looking up at the frieze of little pictures.'

Both women look up at the pictures, all the same size, which hang on the wall side by side, just beneath the ceiling.

'Why does each one depict an apple?' asks the customer.

'Because of Turing. The inventor committed suicide in an odd way. On the seventh of June 1954, he soaked an apple in a solution of cyanide and placed it on a small table. Next, he painted a picture of it, and then he ate the apple.'

'He never did!'

'It's said that this is the reason why the Apple Macintosh logo depicts an apple with a bite out of it. It's Alan Turing's apple.'

'Well, well . . . at least I won't die an idiot.'

'And when our youngest child was born,' continues Lucrèce, getting back to business, 'we put together this suicide kit.'

'What is it?' The interested customer comes closer.

Madame Tuvache shows her the item. 'In this transparent plastic wallet, you can see that you have a little canvas mounted on a stretcher, two brushes – one large, one fine – a few tubes of paint and of course the apple. Careful, it's poisoned! This way, you can kill yourself just like Alan Turing did. The only thing we ask of you, if you don't have any objection, is that you leave us the painting. We really love hanging them up there. They act as souvenirs for us. And, besides, it's pretty, seeing all those apples in a line under the ceiling. They go well with the Delft tiles on the floor. We already have seventy-two of them. While people wait at the cash register, they can look at the exhibition.'

This is exactly what the fat customer is doing. 'They are painted in all kinds of styles . . .'

'Yes, some apples are Cubist, others almost abstract. The blue apple, there, was painted by a man who was colour-blind.'

'I shall take the suicide kit,' sighs the fat lady, her heart beating out a funeral march. 'It will add to your collection.'

'You're very kind. Try and remember to sign and date it. The date today is –'

'What time is it?' asks the customer.

'A quarter to two.'

'I must go. I don't know if it's from seeing all the fruit in your frieze, but I'm feeling a little peckish now.'

As Madame Tuvache opens the door for her, she warns: 'Make sure you don't eat the apple until you've finished the painting! You're not supposed to paint the core. In any case, you wouldn't have time.'

*

Mishima is sitting on a stool at the back of the shop, stirring a basin containing a mixture of cement, sand and water. Alan comes down the stairs, whistling a merry tune. His father asks him: 'Ready to go back to school for the afternoon? Did you finish your lunch, and remember to watch the news on TV?'

'Yes, Father. The lady presenter on the one o'clock bulletin has changed her hairstyle. She looked very well groomed.'

His mother rolls her eyes heavenwards and cuts in: 'Is that all you remember? That's a real worry. Didn't she talk about regional wars, ecological disasters, famine . . . ?'

'Oh yes, we saw those pictures again of the Dutch dykes that exploded during the last tidal wave, and the beach that now extends as far as Prague. They showed the emaciated inhabitants of the German province crying out and rolling naked in the dunes. If you narrowed your eyes, the shining grains of sand mixed with the sweat on their skin looked like little stars. It was unreal but everything will be sorted out. They're going to remove the sand.'

Lucrèce is at her wits' end. 'Oh, you! With your optimism, you'd make a desert bloom! Go on, get off to school. I have more than enough to do without forever seeing you as happy as a lark.'

'See you soon, Mother!'

'Yes, soon, that's right. Unfortunately . . .'

Mishima, who is next to the fresh produce section currently under construction, rolls up one sleeve of his jumper. He pours water onto his forearm, then sand, and turns his arm around under the light from the neon tubes, at the same time screwing up his eyes.

His wife looks at him. 'What on earth are you doing?'

13

'It's a cement breeze-block with a ring attached. It comes with a chain, which you padlock to your ankle. You stand beside the river. You throw it in front of you and – *splash!* You're dragged down to the bottom and it's all over.'

'That's interesting,' nods a customer with a moustache.

Mishima runs the palm of his hand across his brow and half of his bald pate, then continues: 'I make them myself here or in the cellar, with the name of the shop moulded in relief on one side. Pass your hand over it. It reads: THE SUICIDE SHOP. These breeze-blocks can also be used for defenestration.'

The customer is astonished. As he looks at him, Mishima gives a lop sided smile plumping his cheek out on one side under eyes as round as marbles. He raises his eyebrows. 'Yes, yes, yes, breeze-blocks make you heavier because before, you know, on nights when there was a tornado or a hurricane, and people with light bodies threw themselves out of the window, they were found the next morning in their pyjamas, having ended up stuck ridiculously in the branches of a tree, hanging from lampposts or stretched out on a neighbour's balcony. Whereas with the Suicide Shop breeze-block fixed to your ankle, you fall straight down.'

'Ah!'

'Often in the evening, I lift the curtain in our bedroom and watch them falling from the estate's towers. With the breeze-block on one ankle, they look like shooting stars. When there are a lot of them, on nights when the local sports team gets beaten, you'd think it was sand flowing down from the towers. It's pretty.'

Standing anxiously beside the cash register, Lucrèce knits her brows above her beautiful dark eyes, observes her husband, listens to him, and wonders:

'Could Alan be contagious?'

14

'You want to die? Kiss me.'

Marilyn Tuvache sits enthroned like a queen in the fresh produce section. Seated in a large armchair, upholstered in scarlet velvet and carved with gilded acanthus leaves, she wears a clinging dress with a plunging neckline. She leans towards a customer who is intimidated by her new splendour, her youth and the blondeness of her hair. Her lipsticked mouth pouts towards the despairing client: 'Here, on the mouth, with your tongue . . .'

The customer dares to approach. Marilyn unfurls her large square of white silk – Alan's gift – and uses it to cover her own and the man's head. And beneath the scarf, which hangs down below their shoulders and conjures up images of ghosts, you can just make out that they're kissing. The heads move slowly for a long time beneath the silk, then Marilyn pulls it away. A delicate thread of saliva stretches between their mouths. The customer collects it with the back of one hand, then licks it so as not to lose anything.

'Thank you, Marilyn . . .'

'Don't linger. Other customers are waiting.'

Marilyn Tuvache's new post is proving to be a success, much to the amazement of her parents.

'After a school career that was doomed from the very beginning, she has finally found her place . . . in the fresh produce section,' sighs her mother.

'It's the best idea we've had since the Alan Turing kit,' confirms her father.

And the till drawer pings shut. There's a waiting list. When customers telephone to reserve a Death Kiss, Lucrèce replies: 'Yes of course, but not before next week!'

There are so many candidates for the Death Kiss that checks have to be made to ensure that customers don't come back several times. Some of them complain: 'But I'm not dead yet!'

'Ah, well, the Death Kiss can take time to work but it will come and, besides, you can only have one go or there won't be enough to go round.'

Some suicidal customers ask if, by paying more, they could spend an entire night with Marilyn.

Lucrèce is offended by this: 'And then what next? We're not procurers, you know!'

Indignantly, Mishima kicks them out of his shop. 'Go on, get lost! We don't need customers like you here.'

'But I want to die.'

'Sort out your own mess. Go to the tobacconist's shop!'

And, at the back of the shop, Marilyn blossoms like an exotic, carnivorous flower as she kisses the men.

Alan passes close by her, whistling under his breath. 'You see, I was right when I said you were beautiful! All the guys in the City of Forgotten Religions estate are only interested in you. Look at them . . .'

They are waiting, the young men from the Osiris tower who've obtained a group discount. In single file between the display units they move forward centimetre by centimetre, through the shelving with its forests of familiar symbols – a skull for toxic products, a black cross on an orange background for noxious and irritant substances, a drawing of a tilted test tube and a droplet to signify corrosives, a black circle with lines emerging from it in star formation indicating explosives, a flame symbolising flammable products and a leafless tree beside a dead fish showing that a product is harmful to the environment. Triangles are illustrated with a lightning flash, an exclamation mark, another skull and then three circles joined together for biological dangers. Every one of the items for sale here is decorated with one of these symbols, but now none of the male customers seems to want anything but a kiss from Marilyn. Jealous female customers are sulking a little.

'But ...! You can partake too, ladies,' points out Mishima, who is broad-minded. 'Marilyn has nothing against it.'

A nice young man enters the overcrowded shop, declaring that he has made a booking for a Death Kiss. Lucrèce turns her gaze towards him:

'*You*'ve been before. I recognise you.'

'No, I've never been.'

'Yes, you have; I've seen you before.'

'I'm the warden from the cemetery where your daughter used to lay wreaths for the customers who invited you to their funerals.'

'Oh, forgive me!' exclaims Lucrèce, suddenly lifting a hand to her mouth in confusion. 'I couldn't place you. And yet I should have, because, apart from the cemetery, we don't get out much. Sometimes at the weekend we go to the woods to pick poisonous mushrooms, but apart from that ... It's all these customers trying to come several times who are making my head spin.'

The delicate young man gets into the queue behind them. He is desperate, infinitely wise, and as pale as a candle. His attractive face ravaged by cancers of the heart, he observes Marilyn's breasts in her low-cut dress as she bends forward, and the way her neckline gapes open when she twists round to kiss the men. He gazes fearfully at the woman who is about to give him a kiss. When his turn comes, he commands: 'Poison me, Marilyn.'

Wiping her lips, Marilyn Tuvache looks at him and replies:

'No.'

15

'What do you mean, no?' demands her mother in astonishment, hands on her hips at the back of the store.

'Yes, why not?' repeats her father in his cable-knit waistcoat, pushing his way through the crowd to find out what's happening with Marilyn: 'Has she broken down?'

'I will not kiss that boy,' his daughter tells him.

'But why? What's wrong with him? He seems quite nice and he's a good-looking lad. You've kissed uglier ones, and ones who seemed unpleasant in other ways too.'

The young man in question stands facing young, blonde Marilyn Tuvache, seated on her throne. He can't take his eyes off her. 'I never see you any more, Marilyn,' he says. 'You don't come to the cemetery any more. Kiss me.'

'No.'

'Oh, come on, you have to sort this out,' scolds Monsieur Tuvache. 'Customers are waiting. Marilyn, kiss the boy!'

'No.'

Mishima is stunned. Lucrèce, who is standing beside him, shakes her head.

'Oh, *I* see . . .'

She takes her husband to one side, next to the staircase and beyond the range of indiscreet ears. 'Your daughter is in love. After kissing all and sundry, it was bound to happen one day . . .'

'What are you saying, Lucrèce?'

'She's in love with that young cemetery warden, and so she doesn't want to give him a kiss.'

'He's the cemetery warden? I didn't recognise him. Well, all the same, it's idiotic. When you're in love, you kiss.'

'Come, come, Mishima, think! She has the Death Kiss.'

'Shit . . .' Her husband, who had forgotten this, pales and, with the ground taken away from under his feet, he sits down on one of the steps of the staircase and gazes at the refrigerated section. 'If it's not death-cap mushrooms going rotten here or the golden frogs escaping, it's Marilyn falling in love. This fresh produce section is cursed.'

The crowd in the shop grumbles and grows impatient.

'Hey, are we going to get some service . . . ?'

Mishima gets up, goes over to the young cemetery warden and proposes an arrangement.

'Wouldn't you rather have a rope or some poison? There are ways of finishing with life, especially here! Razorblades, the Turing apple – doesn't that appeal to you? Lucrèce, what could we offer him? And for you, sir, it would be a gift! It doesn't matter what, a tanto and a kimono, whatever you want, but decide!'

'I want Marilyn to kiss me.'

'No,' replies the Tuvaches' daughter. 'I love you, Ernest.'

'And I love you too,' says the cemetery warden. 'To death.'

It's an impasse. Despite the crowd, a deathly silence has now fallen over the shop, when suddenly it's broken by the sound of shouting.

16

'*Boom Boom. Fiddledy-dee! And that's the way we do it! That's the way we do it, that's the way we do it! That's the way we do it here!*'

'What on earth is that?!'

Monsieur Tuvache raises his head towards the ceiling, for the song, sung at full volume, seems to come from upstairs.

'*Boom Boom. Fiddledy-dee!*'

Madame Tuvache clenches her teeth. Nerves pulse, and make her cheeks hollow. She purses her lips so hard they whiten. The phials of poison tremble and knock against each other on the shelves. With the vibrations of the ear-splitting song, they quiver and start to move around, even fall. Lucrèce rushes forward to hold them back.

'This is Alan's doing!'

A neon tube blows, emitting an acrid-smelling skein of smoke that pricks the eyes of all the candidates for suicide who are waiting for a Death Kiss from Marilyn. A seppuku sabre, attached to the wall above the stairs, comes loose, plummeting to the ground tip-first, and buries itself in a step. Its glistening blade vibrates and throws out flashes of light while the ropes for hanging uncoil and fall onto the tiled floor, where the customers' feet get tangled up in slip-knots. Mishima can't cope. The jar of sweets on the counter falls off and shatters into a thousand sparkling fragments of glass. The razorblades slide away. The little paintings with Turing's apple on them fall down, and you'd think you were standing under an apple tree and someone was shaking the trunk. The drawer of the cash register opens all by itself, displaying all the banknotes recently brought in by the fresh produce section. Dishonest folk from Buddha's tower grab handfuls of them.

Seeing this pillage, Mishima orders loud and clear: 'Right, everyone out! It'll be dark soon anyway. You can die another time. Keep your numbered tickets and come back tomorrow when everything has been tidied up! And that means you too, young warden . . . Go on, get a move on, outside! Take this one-shot disposable revolver and don't come back to bug us with all that talk about love.'

'*Boom Boom. Fiddledy-dee! That's the way we do it!*'

Expelled depressives emerge from the shop, mechanically humming: '*Boom Boom. Fiddledy-dee . . .*' while all the neon tubes are now winking on and off like the spotlights above the dance-floor at the Kurt Cobain discotheque.

'Alan, will you turn that music off?' shouts his mother, but her younger son upstairs can't hear for the din of the two hundred soldier singers – tenors, baritones and solid bass voices – of the Red Army choir, singing at the tops of their voices: '*Boom Boom. Fiddledy-dee!*' and clicking their heels as well.

Lucrèce abandons the phials she was holding in place, so they rain down, their toxins exploding all over the tiled floor and trickling under the gondolas.

'At least it'll rid the place of rats.'

As she climbs the stairs she is surprised to have had this thought. She enters Alan's room.

'For goodness' sake, will you stop that racket?'

'*Boom Boom. Fidd*—' Click!

Lucrèce has just turned off the sound. 'You're sick, that's what you are! We were reliving a Greek tragedy in the fresh produce section, and this is the music you put on, you imbecile!' she yells. 'And there's your brother, did you think about your brother? I bet he's destroyed every-thing again because of having to listen to your stupid songs . . .' she continues, walking out into the corridor and entering Vincent's room.

Vincent is facing his intact model stoically,

tapping his fingernails on the table to the rhythm of '*Boom Boom. Fiddledy-dee.*'

His mother approaches his bandaged cranium, and her haunted eyes peer at the construction in astonishment. 'Huh? You've joined up the rails of your Big Dipper?'

'It was Alan who told me it would be better and that the people would be happier . . .'

'So this brilliant concept becomes a bog-standard theme park! And what's more, my cooking is burning in the oven. Come on, everyone, get yourselves round that table!'

Mishima, who has pulled down the steel shutters but left the door open to let some air in, switches off the lights. His daughter, who's already at the top of the stairs, is dragging her feet again. He begins to grope his way up the steps in the dark, stops, switches on the bulb above him. On the landing, Alan looks at him and smiles.

His mother, who's in a foul mood, comes charging out of the kitchen and bangs a dish down on the dining-room table. 'And I don't want to hear any comments, all right? With all this trouble going on, I cooked the best I could.'

'What is it?' asks Vincent.

'The leg of a lamb that threw itself off the cliffs. That's why the bone is broken. The butcher saved it for me. But what's it to you? You're anorexic. Mishima, your plate!'

'I'm not hungry,' warns Marilyn.

The atmosphere at the table is dark and brooding. Marilyn snivels, and everyone is sulking except Alan, who is in ecstasies: 'Wow, this is really good, Mother!'

Lucrèce raises her eyes to the heavens and says irritably: 'What do you mean it's good, you cretin? I did any old thing! I started off roasting it, then I put some foil on it as if it was a fish *en papillote*, so what are you saying? I even sprinkled it with sugar before I noticed that I had meant to season it with salt and pepper.'

'Ah, I see ...' smiles Alan's cheerful, hungry face. 'That's where that slightly caramelised taste comes from. And then you covered it with aluminium foil, what a good idea! So it's crisp on the outside and soft and succulent inside.'

Vincent, who is wearing the expression of Van Gogh in a crisis, pushes his plate towards the food. Monsieur and Madame Tuvache look at each other. Lucrèce serves her elder son while her younger one applauds her: 'You should open a restaurant. It would be better than the one opposite, the François Vatel, and the customers would be so delighted that they'd come back often.'

'It's not my vocation to feed people; that's a poor task. I poison them and they never come back! When will you ever accept that?'

Alan laughs: 'That's more or less what they do at the Vatel ... That's why they're closing down soon. You're pretending to be cross, but I know that deep down you're glad I think your roast lamb's good.'

'It is true – it's first-rate,' Monsieur Tuvache is forced to acknowledge.

His wife looks daggers at him: 'So you're on his side too, Mishima?'

Vincent wipes his cracked lips then pushes his plate towards the roast a second time. He serves himself a large portion. Lucrèce puts down her knife and fork. Only Marilyn looks disgusted and doesn't touch hers.

'I understand,' her mother says to her confidingly. 'At least one person in the family has taste.' Lucrèce looks round at the others. 'She doesn't talk nonsense. She wouldn't waste her saliv–'

'Waaaaah!' The blonde blubbers into her porcelain plate.

'What? What did I say?' cries her mother as she sees a look of reproach in her husband's eyes.

'Waaah! Mother, Father ... I can't ever kiss Ernest, the boy I love, or I'll kill him!'

'He's called Ernest?' asks Mishima. 'Like Hemingway? Apparently Hemingway's mother sent him the Smith & Wesson revolver he used for his suicide along with a chocolate cake. His father had already shot himself and his granddaughter did too, on the thirty-fifth anniversary of the writer's suicide. He'd demanded that she was called Margaux because that was the name of his favourite wine. She became an alcoholic and screwed everything up! That's amusing, don't you think?'

This time it's Lucrèce who frowns at her husband, who goes on: 'All right, maybe not. It's true that this Death Kiss thing's a bit unfortunate. Damn, a good lad who could have given us grandchildren and who has a career with a future: a cemetery warden! Because Vincent and children, I don't think ... And as for the other one, if he gets married one day, it'll be to a clown. And, well, if I have to have circus artistes in the shop, juggling with phials of poison or making hula hoops out of hangmen's ropes, it's not worth it ...'

Vincent Tuvache is concentrating, chewing like a ruminant. Before, the mere idea of swallowing food made him vomit the bile from his empty stomach, but here he is, feasting, chewing at length and appreciating the juices of the suicidal lamb as they flow down his throat. Seated next to Alan, he asks him with a full mouth: 'Is it three times you have to sing *Boom* before *fiddledy-dee*?'

'No, twice,' replies his brother: '*Boom Boom. Fiddledy-dee.*'

Their mother, who is sitting opposite Vincent, is thunderstruck by the boys' indifference to their sister's despair. Crushed, she listens as her youngest child advises her while wiping his plate with some bread:

'I was thinking that maybe ... with some roundels of banana too, placed in the lamb juices to pickle, and then some orange zest sprinkled on the juices ...'

Lucrèce contemplates her child and finds only cause for regret: 'Why, oh why did we test a condom with a hole in it?'

Seated to her left and facing Alan, Marilyn starts blubbering again and censures her parent:

'And what about me, Mother, why did you want me to have death in my mouth like a rattle-snake? You never think about the future!'

'The thing is ... preparing for the future, we ... given our profession ...' apologises Monsieur Tuvache at the end of the table. 'We're more accustomed to the short term, if I can put it like that.'

Lucrèce has had enough, and spits out words in a tone she's never used for her eldest before: 'Vincent, stop stuffing yourself! It's indecent. Your sister is in pain!'

'Really, why?' asks Alan.

Mishima looks at the long knife used to cut up the meat, then locates the exact spot on his youngest child's chest where he would have to plunge it for a seppuku. He is feeling murderous, but regains control of himself and reminds Alan in a neutral voice: 'Since she came of age, your sister is poisonous –'

'No, she's not!' sniggers the Tuvaches' youngest child. 'For her birthday, I opened the fridge and replaced the filth in the syringe with a glucose solution, like the doctor uses for Vincent when he's too weak. What do you think?'

A deathly silence descends, giving us a moment to observe the style of the dining room: a violet sofa (the colour of mourning) in front of the curtained window overlooking the City of Forgotten Religions, an old sideboard dating perhaps from the twenty-first century, a lamp-shade in the shape of Saturn with its rings above the table, and at the back, in a corner, a 3D television, which during the news makes you believe that the woman presenter is actually physically in the dining room with you to give you the news of all the ghastly catastrophes in person.

'What did you say, Alan?'

'Did you know this, Vincent?'

'Yes,' belches the Tuvaches' eldest child, wiping his lips with his napkin.

The parents are stunned. This reminds Lucrèce of the time she breathed in a little Sandman by accident. She thinks she's going to faint.

Marilyn is still not entirely sure she has understood properly. 'What exactly are you saying?'

His breathing slow and laboured, her father growls like a storm appearing on the horizon, laden with acid rain: 'You can go back to your cemetery warden. Go on, Marilyn! Your kisses are inoffensive and, without knowing, you have deceived the customers . . .'

Mishima's voice swells: '. . . And all because these two little scum . . . !'

Lightning flashes from his eyes.

'. . . slipped you a placebo.'

His tongue claps within his mouth like thunder.

'Doing such a thing . . . Tuvaches! You are the shame of the nation! Ten generations in suicide, and we've never seen such fraud! When they came back, I too was saying, "Why aren't they dying?" And *you*, Vincent! I was so proud of you . . . I should have named you Brutus! You allowed yourself to be influenced by this little bastard who really does deserve to bear the name of an English homosexual. Oh, the little bugger!'

'Come on, Mishima, you're getting everything mixed up!' cuts in Madame Tuvache, who has regained her composure.

But her husband gets to his feet and reaches out his big suicide-broker's paws for Alan's neck, and Alan runs away, laughing, down the corridor, pursued by his father. Marilyn also leaves the table and runs after her young brother. The two chase Alan: one – Mishima – to strangle him, the other – Marilyn – to wrap her arms round him and cry, 'Oh, Alan!'

Her mother, who has not yet quite digested all the recent information, begs: 'Marilyn! Don't kiss your brother, especially if you love him!'

Vincent, seated opposite her, reminds her: 'But, Mother, since it's glucose solution she has in her veins . . .'

'Oh goodness me yes, well, I'll be . . . !'

17

The next morning the cuckoo clock on the wall between the front door of the shop and the window next to the counter reads eight o'clock. Above its enamelled-iron dial the Grim Reaper appears – a skeleton in lime-tree wood, dressed in a long white robe and holding a scythe in his hand – and he sings: 'Cuckoo! Cuckoo!'

The shop's radio switches on automatically for the news: 'After the fracture of the San Andreas fault near Los Angeles, and the series of volcanic eruptions that spread their lava and ash all over the continent in the last century, life is returning to America. Iranian scientists have detected the first signs that lichen is appearing on the former site of New York since the Big One. Sport: another defeat for the regional tea—'

Lucrèce, in apron and gas mask, is sluicing away the poisons that fell onto the floor the previous day, and wonders out loud: 'Won-won-won, won-won-won?'

Mishima turns off the news on the radio. 'What are you saying?'

His wife unfastens some straps and removes

the filtration cartridge from her mask. 'What are we going to do with Marilyn? Either she goes on as if nothing has happened or she stops. I won't hide the fact that I would regard that as a shame, for it brought a sudden boost to sales in the fresh produce section. Close the drawer of the cash register, Mishima.'

Her husband does so, then puts back the ropes thoughtfully. He sweeps up, using a dustpan and brush to collect the fragments of the broken jar and the sweets, which he empties onto the counter in a heap. Then he orders Alan: 'Pick out the bits of glass from this confectionery. We can't have the children cutting their tongues! And watch yourself too, don't cut yourself on a fragment. I don't know ...' he admits to his wife.

Marilyn is wearing her work dress: a lamé creation with a plunging neckline, which clings to her body. She raises her arms, which tantalisingly accentuates the flawless flow of her curves, the perfect arch of her back, her smooth, tensed belly, her outrageously rounded buttocks, her curved breasts high up because she is perched at the top of a ladder, re-hanging the last of the little paintings from the frieze of apples.

'There, that's done! While you're having a think, I've got almost an hour before we open to go and see if Ernest has arrived at the cemetery and tell him the good news.'

'Oh, damn!' exclaims Mishima, who is under the ladder.

His daughter thinks she has dropped a picture on his head. She bends down to him. 'What?'

Her father strikes the top of his bald forehead with the palm of his hand. 'I did something stupid . . .'

Lucrèce, who is wearing surgical gloves and rinsing a floor-cloth in a bucket, straightens up. 'What?'

'Yesterday evening, in a panic, I gave Ernest a disposable Smith & Wesson.'

'What?!'

Madame Tuvache is stunned, and Marilyn's feet slip off the step on the ladder to glide down the uprights to the floor. Her stretchy dress, which was so sexy a moment ago, suddenly puffs out, swelling up like a ridiculous parachute.

'But, Father, we have to do something!'

'What?'

'Last night with your revolver . . . m-my love' – she stammers at the thought of it – 'he may have sho– he may have sho–'

'What?

Her stupefied father does not want to hear her

spell it out, while Lucrèce takes off her surgical gloves and takes matters in hand:

'I know what we are going to do, Mishima.'

'What?'

'Go quickly to the Tristan and Isolde florist, and ask if they've seen him go past this morning, while I go to his mother's place in the Moses tower. Marilyn, run to the cemetery and as for you' – she calls to Alan – 'while you're waiting for us to come back and open up, you're in charge of the shop.'

Alan turns round in astonishment:

'What?'

18

It is almost nine o'clock as Lucrèce and Mishima return together, but they enter via the small back door of the ancient place of worship, which has become the Suicide Shop. Their youngest child has not heard them coming in, for his ears are blocked by the headphones of a personal stereo, whose buzzing his parents can hear. He's listening to an optimistic song and singing the words to himself as he bustles around:

'It doesn't take much to be happy, really not much to be happy . . . !'

The boy with the curly blond hair is snapping the fingers of his left hand to the beat in front of the window where he's pushed the lucky bags. With his right hand, he lifts up each of the acid drops, looks at it, and throws on average one out of every two into Lucrèce's bucket, where they dissolve amid the poisoned waters.

'It doesn't take much . . . !'

'What's he doing?' whispers Mishima in Lucrèce's ear, and she replies, 'He's spotting which sweets are stuffed with cyanide by how transparent they are, and throwing them away.'

'Oh, the —'

Madame Tuvache puts a hand over her husband's mouth. In his temper, he's lashed out and clumsily dislodged a rolled-up rope at the end of the double central display unit. It flops onto the floor with a dull thud.

Alan, still standing in front of the window, turns round. Baby-faced and dotted with reddish freckles, he removes one earpiece, listens and notices the rope that's fallen on the floor. Leaving the window and still singing to himself, he grabs a razorblade from the display, then goes to pick up the rope and cuts the fibres at random.

'It doesn't take much to be happy! Really not much . . .'

To the rhythm of the song, he makes incisions around the slip-knot, wets one index finger with saliva and slides it over the fibres to hide his sabotage, then puts the rope back among the others. His parents, hiding behind the staircase, are outraged, but they continue to spy on their child, who returns to the counter lisping and dancing a little jig.

'Drive all your worries from your mind! See life on the bright side . . .'

He wears out the razorblade on a breeze-block moulded by his father, then when it's become blunt and useless he puts it back with the others.

He opens several transparent bags from the Alan Turing suicide kits, inside which he replaces the apples with new ones.

'Where did he get those?' whispers Mishima.

'From the fruit basket in the dining room.'

'I hope he's not going to put the other ones in their place . . . Oh, the little devil!'

Monsieur Tuvache emerges, muttering, from beneath the stairs. The Grim Reaper shoots out of the cuckoo clock and announces nine o'clock: 'Cuckoo! Cuckoo . . .!' The radio switches on automatically for the news:

'Weather! Things are getting worse. Sulphuric acid rain is expected . . .'

Monsieur Tuvache switches off the radio and faces his surprised younger son, who takes the earpieces out of his ears in order to hear his parent thunder: 'Right! I've had it with you!'

Up above, on the wall, the Grim Reaper continues to play out his series of nine irritating double 'Cuckoos' indicating the hour. Mishima throws a poisoned apple at the clock. Taking a hit, the Reaper loses his lime-wood head and the fatal fruit becomes impaled upon the blade of the scythe. 'Cuck–!' The apple and the unbalanced, decapitated figure block the little arched doors, preventing them from closing, while the fruit drops its juice onto the Reaper's robe.

Alan's eyes narrow against the blast of Mishima's fatherly wrath. His parent's tongue twists in his mouth like the blades of a fan, and Alan's curls fly back from his sweet little face. 'You will spend your two-week school holiday this winter in Monaco, training as a suicide commando!'

Lucrèce suddenly joins them, holding her head in her hands.

'Oh no, Mishima! Not Monaco. Please not there!'

'Yes!'

The mother of the family pleads with her husband: 'But, darling, the people there are all nutcases, mad with hatred and brutality, whereas he's so ... very ...'

'Maybe they'll put a hole in his head, so his vocation can sink in!' shouts Monsieur Tuvache, who then says to his son: 'Go and get your things ready! Do not take any CDs. This is not a place where they listen to songs – no, that's not what kamikazes do!'

Lucrèce is devastated, but Alan looks on the bright side of this punishment: 'Monaco? Well, it'll be warm there. I'll take some sun cream too, and a pair of trunks in case we go swimming ...'

19

'What on earth is wrong with you, Ernest? You're all pale!'

'Ooooh ... It's that mask! I thought I would die of fright when I saw it,' replies Ernest to his future mother-in-law.

'The mask Vincent designed has that effect on you?' Lucrèce is astonished.

'But why does he build such horrors?' trembles the young cemetery warden, sitting down on a step to try and recover his composure.

'It was my Alan, before he left for his training camp – poor little chap, let's hope ... – who advised him to purge himself of all his anxieties by building masks that represented the monsters from his nightmares.'

'Well, I must say ...'

Marilyn is in raptures. 'My fiancé is so sensitive!' She comes to sit down beside him and takes him in her arms. 'Baby ...'

'Well, I must say, for a cemetery warden ...' comments Mishima, joining them.

'No, but honestly ... Vincent really ought to

warn people!' Marilyn's true love justifies himself. 'Because it's serious . . .'

'Come on,' Lucrèce downplays it, 'he's finally found his appetite and now he never stops stuffing his face. That's real progress. And besides, Ernest, you know that we Tuvaches . . . well, we don't really like psychiatrists very much . . .'

'Yes, but all the same . . . I don't suppose you have a small glass of eau de vie by any chance?'

'Eau de –? Oh no, we don't keep that in stock,' apologises Mishima. 'On the other hand, those masks . . . I'm wondering . . . if they can produce this effect . . . for people who are oversensitive or have a weak heart . . . we'll have to see!' he concludes, as the skeleton door chime begins to tinkle.

A plump, curly-headed lady enters.

'Well, Madame Phuket-Pinson!' trills Lucrèce, heading for her. 'Have you come so that I can pay off our little butcher's account?'

'No, it's not that. It's for me . . .'

'Oh, really? What's going on?'

'I've found out that since I've been ill my husband has been having an affair with the waitress at Vatel's. So I want to put an end to it all. I was already suffering with my health problems . . .'

'Oh yes . . . heart problems, I believe . . .'

murmurs Monsieur Tuvache with false sympathy as he approaches, carrying a carrier bag containing Vincent's mask. 'Now, Madame Phuket-Pinson, close your eyes and don't peep, while I check something out for you . . .'

The rotund, docile butcher's wife, resigned as an animal at the abattoir, lowers her eyelids with their long, cow-like lashes. Mishima ties the cords of the bulky mask behind her neck and head, then hands a mirror to her. 'Now look at yourself.'

Madame Phuket-Pinson opens her eyes and discovers her new appearance in the mirror:

'*Aaargh!*'

Cheeks made from a chicken carcass that Vincent must have retrieved from the kitchen bin and scraped clean, skin made from a worn-out floor-cloth on the forehead and chin, a nose made from the beak of a cackling hen. On either side, the eyes are windmills in green and pink plastic, like the ones which have been sold for centuries around the lakes in parks. They turn round and make music. Two lines of teeth blink on and off – the lights from a battery-powered Christmas tree decoration – between shattered lips made up of bone fragments from a leg of lamb which had suffered an open fracture! Vincent's nights must not be restful ones. The vision of his nightmares terrifies the plump heart patient, who catches sight of the multicoloured tangle of the mask's ample head of hair, dotted with imitation spiders and other poisonous creatures. By means of a clever system, smoke escapes from the eyes and spirals up as the eyes move.

'*Aaargh . . . !*'

The butcher's wife falls to the ground, rigid. Mishima kneels beside her, then leans over: 'Madame Phuket-Pinson? Madame Phuket-Pinson?'

He stands up and has to admit:

'It works!'

20

Marilyn Tuvache poisons through her sweat, at least that's what she says. She shakes customers' hands. 'Death salutes you, sir.'

One scrawny, desperate young man with a mischievous look, the only customer in the shop and standing right in front of her, is surprised – 'Is that all? You think that'll be enough?' – while Marilyn slips the fingers of her right hand into a fleece glove, to make her palm sweat.

'Oh yes, yes,' she replies with aplomb. 'My lethal sweat will have penetrated your pores and soon you will be . . .'

'Can't I have a little kiss from Death too?' the other demands.

'Fine, a little kiss, yes.'

She bends forward, and leaves the sensual imprint of her lipstick on one cheek. The customer shows his disappointment. 'No, but, I meant there, on the mouth, with the tongue and the saliva, like you did before . . . It's so I can be really sure.'

'Oh no, that's finished . . .' The curvaceous blonde sits up on her throne, in her lamé dress.

'Because now I am engaged to the cemetery warden,' she confesses, blushing and fluttering the lashes of her heavily made-up eyes.

The customer, telling himself that he never has any luck, goes to pay at the checkout: 'How much do I owe?'

'Twelve euro-yens.'

'Twelve?! Blimey, some people really earn a good living . . . They shake your hand and they've earned twelve.'

'Yes, but afterwards you're dead,' justifies Monsieur Tuvache.

'Well, I hope so! At that price . . .'

And the customer, whom everything disappoints, leaves, pushing through the little metal tubes of the skeleton that tinkles on the door. Back in the shop, Monsieur Tuvache shakes his head, uncomfortable. Five o'clock on the dot! In the cuckoo clock, the wrecked headless lime-wood figure of the Grim Reaper, which is still stuck between the doors, splutters as he shakes the blade of his scythe, embedded in a mouldy apple. 'Cuck—!'

Mishima lifts his head and comments: 'That clock's ridiculous now . . . And, in any case, nothing here works properly any more.'

The radio switches on: 'Catastrophe! The regional government promises terrorist attacks by our suicide comma—' He switches it off. 'That radio's starting to get on my nerves too.'

'But, darling, you're the one who wanted us to programme it so that it would come on automatically at news time and go off automatically as soon as the songs and variety shows came on. You said that for the custom—'

Lucrèce, sitting anguished at the cash register, chews her lip and wrings her hands in anxiety, because she really wanted to hear the rest of the news to find out what was happening.

Her husband, handsome as a Roman emperor even though he is semi-bald, looks closely at Marilyn at the back of the shop. Wearing her polar fleece glove, she is carelessly flicking through the pages of a women's magazine in the fresh produce section. 'What we're doing isn't honest. My ashamed ancestors must be turning in their graves. And to think that in addition we're now selling comical carnival masks . . . This shop used to have quality; now it's looking more and more like a stall selling jokes and novelties.'

'But it's so that people can die of fright . . .'

'Yes, yes, Lucrèce! And who exactly is going to die? A heart patient on the way out of hospital? They may impress a susceptible cemetery warden, but apart from that . . . You know as well as I do, people buy them from us to amuse everyone at birthday parties.'

'Perhaps they die laughing when they blow out the candles . . .'

'Well, of course, you always have to be right, don't you? And also, if you think I haven't seen you, as soon as my back is turned, sorting through the sweets in the light from the window . . . I'm certain that there isn't a single poisoned one left in that jar! When I go down to the cellar, I can hear you offering handfuls of them to the children, and wiping their eyes with a handkerchief. I hear you telling them: "It'll be all right, it'll be all right. Now be good and go home to your parents. They must be worrying about you." No, no, everything's falling apart and even you are standing in my way, my poor Lucrèce. And I know when everything started to go wrong! Why, oh why, did we want to test a condom with a hole in it? What's that, sellotaped to the cash register in front of you?'

'A postcard from Alan, which came this morning . . .' replies Madame Tuvache nervously.

'Let me see. What picture has he chosen? A hologram of a bomb, good . . . Oh, but, of course, he had to draw a smile on it!'

'Oh yes?'

'Hadn't you noticed it, Lucrèce? Before, you

would have noticed it . . .' continues Mishima, postcard in hand, going down into the cellar towards a sack of cement used for making the drowning or defenestration breeze-blocks. 'Oh, that child; I hope they can sort him out for us . . . or that he'll be a martyr.'

Lucrèce, eaten up inside, chews on her fingernails as she gazes far into the distance.

21

Mishima closes the trapdoor of the cellar behind him, switches on a pale light bulb then walks down the steep staircase, where his soul founders. In his hand he holds Alan's holographic postcard and in the wintry, late-afternoon light from the basement window, with his back against the wall, he reads it:

Dear Mother, Father, I love you . . .

This sends a shaft of light through Mishima's heart. This man who sometimes likes to throw his weight around in the house or upstairs in the shop no longer kicks up a fuss when he's alone in the depths of the cellar, reading his youngest child's words:

Don't worry about me. It'll all be fine . . .

Oh, that eternal optimist, that cheeky monkey!

The day fades, the darkness grows. The sky closes slowly like a box. This is the time when the sorrows of the sick become more bitter still, for the dark night takes them by the throat. Underground, just like the dead, Mishima worships at the altar of his distress and lets out a plaintive cry:

'Alan . . .'

It's little more than a thought and less than a whisper. Breeze-block sand flows through his fingers. It is like cold water rising, it is like a shame that grows. For a week now, every night, he has suffered a terrible nightmare, struggling like a drowning man. In his bed, to left and to right, all he can find is insomnia. And even when he is asleep, he cries:

'Alan!'

Through the cellar's barred window, he hears the sounds of heels on the pavement above. Hemmed in by this monotonous hammering, it sounds as if someone is nailing down a coffin somewhere. It is dusk. The sand turns bluish. It is always evening, more or less, for someone in the world, always a time when someone is frightened. 'I can't take any more,' says the acid rain. 'I can't take any more of all this.' Mishima had thought he was balancing freely on a steel wire when in fact all the balance came from the balancing pole. He misses Alan. Nothing can act as a counterweight. Outside, a shriek from a tram – a finger caught in the electric wires – and deep in the cellar the pervasive feeling of suicides shying away from the brink. The fine sand, vaguely starry. Mishima feels like the breeze-block in front of him – he no longer has any law but his own weight. One of Alan's abandoned shirts rests on a chair. He picks it up, buries his head in it, and voids his sorrow in a great flood of tears.

Did she hear him sobbing? Standing beside the shop's cash register, Lucrèce lifts up the trapdoor and asks in the half-light: 'Mishima, are you all right? Mishima!'

22

'There aren't many customers this morning.'

'Yes, it's dead.'

'Maybe it's because the regional team won yesterday.'

'Maybe ...'

A young tramp enters the Suicide Shop. He is wearing a large, dirty overcoat that fits tightly round him over a mass of ragged knitted jumpers. Stained trousers hang shapelessly down his legs and his feet are enveloped in torn bin bags. He asks in a hoarse, coughing voice: 'I would like to kill myself but I don't know if I have the means. What is your cheapest item?'

Mishima, who's wearing a rust-coloured sleeveless pullover with a V-neck over a petrol-blue shirt, replies: 'Those who can't afford anything usually suffocate themselves with our carrier bags. They are very strong. Here, have a bit of adhesive tape too, to seal it properly round your neck.'

'How much do I owe you?'

'Oh, nothing, nothing ...' Monsieur Tuvache smiles, with a slight tension at the corners of his mouth.

The young tramp with the rotten teeth, beneath a red woolly Chinese hat from which dusty, lifeless hair escapes, laments:

'If I could only have met people as unselfish as you more often, I wouldn't be in this position . . . or if I could have had someone attentive and protective like you for a father . . .'

Hearing this, Mishima becomes irritated: 'That's enough!'

But the grateful homeless man indicates the open carrier bag and persists: 'To thank you, I shall put it on while I'm sitting on the bench opposite. Passers-by will read the name of the shop round my head and it'll get you a bit of business. I'll sort of be your sandwich-man.'

'All right . . .' says Mishima wearily, opening the door and feeling how cold it is outside. 'Come on, out you go quickly, there's a nip in the air!'

Once the door is closed, Monsieur Tuvache, who is both feverish and fevered, folds his arms and rubs his hands on his shirt, from shoulders to elbows, to warm himself up. He moves the lucky bags slightly in front of the window by the cash register, and slides his palm across the misted pane.

Outside, he sees the young tramp walk across to the opposite pavement and sit down on a bench. He sees him slide his head into the bag, arrange its opening around his neck and seal it with adhesive tape. He looks just like a bouquet of flowers in a collar. The bouquet soon begins to struggle. The sealed bag swells, subsides, swells. The name of the shop stands out like the slogan on a rubber balloon: THE SUICIDE SHOP. Legs crossed, hands deep in the pockets of his heavy coat and his head drawn in, he suffocates, leaning to one side. Now you can read the other side of the bag: HAS YOUR LIFE BEEN A FAILURE? LET'S MAKE YOUR DEATH A SUCCESS! The young man falls onto the pavement.

Lucrèce comes up behind her husband as though sliding on rails. She watches too. She's extraordinarily dignified, and the way she carries her head on that bird-like neck is pure nobility. Above her red silk blouse, open at the neck, a brown lock of hair sweeps down over her forehead, giving life to her hairstyle. She looks as if she's in a breeze. Her mouth, a little pursed, relaxes and her dark eyes narrow as if she were having difficulty seeing or as if she were looking at something very far, so very far, in front of her. 'At least there, he doesn't feel the cold.'

'Who?'

Mishima replaces the lucky bags and turns round. Through the shop's ceiling, he can hear convulsive sobs interspersed with sniggers, curses, shouts.

'Vincent is up early creating,' comments his father. 'And hasn't Marilyn come down yet?'

'She's having a lie-in with Ernest,' replies his wife.

'Aaah! Wu! Whua!' Vincent is in his bedroom, wearing his grey djellaba decorated with explosives. He has a headache. 'Alan!' He feels as if his skull is about to explode, as if bits of shattered bone are about to be flung across the room. The incredibly long, thick bandage around his head is now so voluminous that he looks like a fakir with a bearded, imploded face. Vincent — this human wound with the blood-red face of an artist in crisis — has eyes like disembowelled sunflowers, and all his distinctive features are a terrific blaze of burning coals which explode into sparks. Although he has put on a little weight, he is still only nerves and flesh laid bare, the violent first casting of someone shredded by life. He has the face, the colour of overfired brick, of an alien suffering from hallucinations. A wave runs up and down him as he looks at a hideous mask furrowed and squeezed on all sides by his intoxicated brush. The tumult of the diverse incongruous materials of this disguise, the radiance and vibrancy of its hues, and the paint that seems to leap straight from the tube, all puke and cry: 'Alan!' Hanging from the lamp on his work table is a holographic postcard from his little brother, which reads: 'You are the city's artist.'

On the other side of the adjoining wall, in the bedroom to the right, Ernest dances lovingly above Marilyn's belly. He bends over to caress her. And when he feels the liquid of his sweetheart's mouth on his teeth, he drinks it, and tells her: 'You have entered my heart like a knife.' The beauty of their caresses is shrouded in rose-scented vapours. The Tuvaches' daughter moves her lips. In a corner, flowers swoon with rapture. The sounds and scents circle in the air; a melancholy waltz and giddy, painful fever. Marilyn's breasts, like shields, catch flashes of light. These make the cemetery warden stumble over his words as though they were cobbles: 'I-I-I love you!' He embraces her and cradles her soul. The eternal smile of the girl's perfect teeth leads him into uncharted places. To him, she is like a beautiful vessel in full sail. Laying bare her breasts to him and lying with one elbow in the cushions, his bare-chested siren looks resplendent. Fervently in love too, she raises her head and lies back. Pinned up on the wall is a postcard: 'You are the most beautiful of all.'

*

Lucrèce, Marilyn, Mishima, Vincent ... All of them miss Alan; life has no meaning without him.

23

'Cuckoo!'

Monsieur Tuvache looks up in surprise and eyes the shop's clock – 'Gracious me, has it started working again?' – then lowers his gaze.

'Oh, it's you! But what are you doing here?'

In front of the poisons display, Madame Tuvache is wrapping up a phial for an old lady with a twisted body. The misshapen monster that used to be a woman complains: 'Getting old takes such a long time.' It seems that the fragile being, who has become as small as a child, is gently progressing, carrier bag in hand, towards a new cradle. Her tears could fill a river.

Lucrèce turns round. 'Alan!'

Bundle of belongings on one shoulder, hair all over the place, her youngest child is standing beside the cash register and suddenly a ray of summer sunshine seems to pass through the shop. His mother rushes towards him: 'My little one, you're alive!'

His outfit, spectacularly colourful in places, is like a summer flowerbed, and hope seems to shine in through the window. Over in the fresh produce section, Marilyn hastily shakes a customer's hand and gets rid of him. 'Off you go! Death says hello to you too!'

Then she runs towards her little brother, her wide skirt sweeping the air and her heart beating like a drum. 'Alan!'

She kisses him, strokes his cheeks, shakes his hands, slides her bare fingers beneath the child's sweatshirt, touches his skin.

Marilyn's customer is astonished. 'Are you killing your little brother too?'

'What? Of course not!'

The dejected customer pays twelve euro-yens, but doesn't understand. He brushes past Alan, dazzled by the health that radiates like bright light from his arms and his shoulders. He makes his exit behind the downcast grandmother.

Madame Tuvache calls out: 'Vincent! Vincent! Come and see! Alan is back!'

Box of chocolates in hand and munching, Vincent appears at the top of the stairs by the little door leading to the spiral staircase of the old religious building (church, temple, mosque? ...) The north wind, blowing under the door, puffs up the bottom of his djellaba, decorated with atom bombs.

Alan climbs the stairs and embraces his big brother. 'Hey, City's Artist, you've put on weight!'

The latter – this turbaned Van Gogh – peers at his younger brother's sweatshirt, illustrated with a design that intrigues him. It depicts an aquarium with a letter at the bottom reading: *Goodbye*. Above the opening of the glass tank, a goldfish drips and flies away, attached to the string of a balloon. Another fish, which is still in the water, is making bubbles and shouting to him: *No, Brian! Don't do it!*

Vincent doesn't laugh.

'What's that?'

'Humour.'

'Oh.'

Arriving at the bottom of the steps, Mishima throws back his head and shouts up to Alan: 'Why have you come back early?'

'I was sent home.'

The child, who astonishes everyone with his frankness, who is at ease everywhere like the air in the sky and water in the sea, walks down the staircase, his laughter covering it with a triumphal carpet.

'I had a lot of fun there but that annoyed the instructors. And I knew how to make the other pupils who were learning to be human bombs like me relax. When we were sneaking through the darkness, dressed in white sheets and a pointed hood with two holes for the eyes, I told them jokes that made them crack up, all over the cakes of plastic explosive taped to their bellies. While they were peeing in the dunes of Nice, I was gathering desert roses and when I told them they were made of camel's piss mixed with sand and carved by the wind, they thought life was marvellous. They went back singing: "*Boom! My heart goes boom ...!*" The director of the suicide-commando course was devastated. I pretended that I didn't understand any of his technical explanations. He was tearing his hair out and his beard. One morning, when he was at the end of his tether, he put on a belt of explosives, took the detonator in his hand and told me: "Look closely, because I'll only be demonstrating this to you once!" And he blew himself up. I was sent home.'

Mishima first nods his head up and down, in silence. He is like an actor who can't remember the words of his part. Then he shakes it from side to side: 'What on earth are we going to do with you?'

'You mean for the rest of the holidays? He can help me make the poisons!' enthuses Lucrèce.

'And he can make masks with me,' says Vincent from the top of the stairs.

24

'Ha ha! Oh, that's so funny, tee hee! Oh, my stomach's hurting. Ha ha ...! I can't breathe! Oooh ...!'

A small, scrawny man with a moustache and a hat, dressed all in grey, had walked sadly into the shop. Lucrèce had shown him a mask made by Vincent and Alan.

'Oooh! Oooh! Oh, but that's funny! Ha ha ha ...! Oh, that moronic face, oh ...!'

Mishima is sitting slumped on a chair, feeling oppressed. Forearms resting on his parted thighs, with his fingers interlaced between his knees, he raises his head with an effort to look at this morning customer, the first of the day. He watches him face-on, guffawing at the sight of the mask Lucrèce is showing him, with her back to her husband.

The laughing customer puts a hand to his mouth. 'Oh! But how could anyone have given birth to that?! Oh!'

'My boys made this mask last night. It's well put together, don't you think?'

'Oh! But what a stupid-looking face. And the

eyes! Tee hee! And nose! Oh good grief, look at the nose . . . I can't believe it!'

The customer bends double with laughter at the sight of the facial disguise, which Madame Tuvache is holding at chest height right in front of him. He's suffocating, coughing, belching.

'Oh no, I mean, really, living with a face like that! It's not the kind of mug to win you friends, is it? And what about women? Do you know a single woman who'd want anything to do with a guy like that? Oh! Not even a dog or a rat would want him!'

The customer laughs until he cries, attempting to get his breath back. 'Show me again. Oh, I can't take any more!'

'Then look away,' Madame Tuvache advises him.

'No, my decision is made. Ha ha ha! And how seedy-looking he is. He must be some kind of bloody idiot, that guy there! Even a goldfish would rather fly out of its bowl than stay looking at him! Aaaah!'

The customer laughs so much he wets himself:

'Oh, forgive me! I'm so embarrassed. I'd heard that you had grotesque masks but this one . . . Aaah!'

'Would you like to see others?' suggests Lucrèce.

'Oh no, nothing could be worse than the one you've shown me. Ha ha! Oh, the idiot! I hope he dies, the damn fool! Nobody will miss the bloody idiot!'

Up to now, Mishima's gaze has been vague and demoralised. Now, he fixes his attention on the unusual customer who is killing himself with laughter at the mask.

'My heart! Aaaah . . . ! Oh, how stupid he looks! Ha ha ha!'

He turns red, becomes rigid, arms folded across his chest and his fingers outspread like the points of a star, then collapses onto the floor, yelling at the mask. 'Idiot!'

Mishima stands up and checks him over:

'Well, that makes two . . . But what did they dream up this time?'

Lucrèce turns round and shows him a mask in impersonal white plastic, onto whose nose Alan and Vincent have stuck a mirror.

25

'Learn to look at yourself using the reflection of this mask, Mademoiselle. Look at yourself again and then take it back to your house. You can put it in your bathroom or on your bedside table.'

'Oh, goodness me, no thank you! I've already seen enough horrors . . .'

'Yes,' insists Alan, facing the cash register. 'Learn to love yourself. Go on, one more time to please me.'

He holds up the mirror mask in front of the young woman, who quickly turns her head away.

'I can't.'

'But why?'

'I'm monstrous.'

'How are you monstrous? What on earth are you saying? You're like everyone else: the same number of ears, eyes, a nose . . . What's the difference?'

'You must be able to see it, little one. My conk is long and misshapen. My peepers are too close together, and I have enormous cheeks, covered in spots.'

'Oh come on, what rubbish! Let's see . . .'

Alan opens the drawer beneath the cash register and unrolls a metre-long dressmaker's tape measure. He places the metal tip of one end between the customer's eyes and stretches it to the tip of the nose. 'Right, seven centimetres. How many should it be? Five? And what about the space between your eyes? Let's measure that. How much further apart should they be? One centimetre, no more. The cheeks ... how much too big are they? Don't move, while I place this under your earlobe. Personally, I'd say four centimetres too big.'

'Each.'

'Yes, each, if you like. But, anyway, it all adds up to a few millimetres compared to the size of the universe. It's not enough to mess everything up! What I know is, when I saw you come in, I didn't see an extra terrestrial with eight tentacles covered in suckers and round eyes at the end of twelve-metre antennae! Ah, you're smiling ... Smiling suits you. See how much it suits you,' he says, lifting up the white plastic mask in front of the customer, who immediately pulls a face.

'My teeth are hideous.'

'No, they're not hideous. Crooked like that, they give you the look of a little girl who's not ready for braces. It's touching. Smile.'

'You're kind.'

'It's true that he's being kind . . .' a low voice comments in a whisper, quite a long way from the young woman's back, 'because her teeth are really terrible.'

'Shh.'

Mishima and Lucrèce, standing side by side by the razorblade rack with arms folded, silently observe their son, who is attempting to flog a mask to this customer, of whom they can see nothing but her waist less back, and her fat bottom, and her legs like fence-posts. They have a glimpse of the ugly features of her inelegant face reflected in the mirror of the white mask as Alan holds it out in front of her.

'Smile. What's happening to you is normal. I've often heard people here say that they began by not being able to look at themselves in shop windows any more, then that they tear up the photos of themselves. Smile, people are looking at you!'

'I'm covered in spots.'

'Anxiety spots . . . When you are more relaxed, they will go away.'

'My colleagues think I'm stupid.'

'That's because you lack confidence in yourself. And that makes you awkward, makes you say the wrong things at the wrong time. But if you gradually reconcile yourself with the

reflection in this mask and learn to love it ...
Look at her, this person in front of you. Look at
her. Don't be ashamed of her. If you met her in
the street, would you want to kill her? What has
she done to be hated so much? What is she guilty
of? Why isn't she loved? If you start to feel
friendly towards this woman yourself, maybe
others will follow suit!'

'Good grief, all that for a hundred euro-yen
mask! I must admit he has a good sales pitch
though, and he really puts his back into selling,'
says Mishima appreciatively.

The disconcerted young woman looks to right
and left.

'Have I made a mistake? I am in the Suicide
Shop, aren't I?'

'Oh, forget it, forget that word; it doesn't lead
anywhere.'

'Why is he saying that?' demands Alan's
father, frowning.

'Life is the way it is. It's worth what it's worth!
It does its best, within its limitations. We mustn't
ask too much of life, either. Nor should we want
to suppress it! It's best to look on the bright side.
So leave the rope and the disposable revolver here.
The way you are at the moment, stressed out and
in a panic, you'll fire into the slip-knot. Anything
could happen. You'll fall off the stool and break

your knee. You don't have pain in your knee, do you?'

'I have pain everywhere.'

'Yes, but in your knee?'

'No, fortu—'

'Well, so much the better! Carry on like that. And may your knee make efforts to carry you back to your tower, with this woman's face on the mask. If you don't do it for me, do it for her. What's her name?'

The customer opens her eyes and looks at the mirror. 'Noémie Ben Sala-Darjeeling.'

'That's a pretty first name, Noémie ... Lovely Noémie. You'll see; she's nice. Take her mask home with you. Smile at her, she'll smile at you. Take care of her, she needs affection. Wash her, dress her in nice clothes, put a little scent on her so that she feels more at home in her skin. Try to accept her. She will become your friend, your confidante, and you will become inseparable. How you will laugh together! And all that for a hundred euro-yens. It's really not expensive. Go on, I'll wrap her up. I'll entrust her to you. Take the greatest care of her. She deserves it.'

At the sound of the till opening, Mishima laments: 'He could at least have billed her for the rope and the revolver as well ...'

'Come on, choose a sweet from the jar,' smiles Alan.

'Oh, aren't they . . . ?' asks the customer.

'Oh no! Off you go. Goodbye, lady who doesn't even have pain in her knee!'

26

When Lucrèce looks straight ahead, her fingers linked on the top of her head, her bent arms make the shape of an eye, with her head as the pupil. On either side of her ears, inside the space left by her arms, the wall behind her gleams like the white of the eye. Madame Tuvache becomes one large fixed eye atop a woman's torso.

'See you again, sir.'

Alan, who is standing next to her, is surprised. 'Gosh, Mother, are you saying "see you again" to the customers now?'

'He didn't buy anything. I said "see you again" because he'll be back. When someone comes in here to look, they always come back sooner or later to buy. They have to get to grips with the idea. Those who are tempted by hanging begin by going out wearing scarves, which they tie more and more tightly. Those kind of people put a hand tightly round their throat to feel the vertebrae, the cartilage, the tendons, the muscles, the throbbing veins. They get accustomed to the feel of it. He'll be back . . .'

Lucrèce, hands still interlinked on her hair,

turns her head and inclines it to the right. And it looks as if the entire large eye is commanding the child. 'Pull down the shutters and turn off the lights. We're going upstairs, Alan.'

27

The door is closed and Mishima is standing at the window of the parental bedroom. Holding the curtain back with one hand, he is watching the sun drowning in its own blood and his life's philosophy falling away in large sections on the balconies of the towers. The future, in freefall, is mortally wounded and, down below, men and their dreams lie shattered.

Monsieur Tuvache, a shopkeeper who has become yellow and melancholic, with the colours of the sunset reflected in his eyes, feels desolate, decrepit, dusty, dirty, abject, slimy, cracked.

He is even growing disenchanted with Lucrèce. Everything is falling apart at the seams, even love and beauty, ready for oblivion to cast them into eternity. He would like to get drunk, but alcohol is expensive, and as for the carnal act, that's yet another thing that is too tiring to contemplate. People say it is entertaining but it's merely a strange sort of gymnastics. And his thoughts go round in his mind to the sound of the hullabaloo.

There are no longer any seasons, no more rainbows, and the snow has given up. Behind the towers of the City of Forgotten Religions – which is a state of mind – are the first large sand dunes, grains from which sometimes blow onto Boulevard Bérégovoy and even under the door of the Suicide Shop. On the ground, whirling, fantastical searchlights sweep through the pollution and the overcast sky with long cones of green light. Birds that venture here on a sudden whim are asphyxiated or die of heart attacks above the towers. In the morning, women collect their feathers and use them to make themselves exotic hats before they too cast themselves into the void.

It is the time of day when shouts come from the immense stadium, suddenly illuminated, and from the population that loves the deadening whip. It is the time of day when, elsewhere, swarms of bad dreams make the first people to fall asleep twist and turn on their pillows. Alas, everything is ruined – action, desire, dreams – and as Mishima holds back the curtain, feeling the air blow in under the window, all the hairs on his arm stand on end with fear. The bedroom door opens and Lucrèce asks: 'Are you coming down to dinner, Mishima?'

'No, I'm not hungry.'

Being alive takes so long. Giving up everything takes so long.

'I'm going to bed.'

The thing is, tomorrow he'll have to live again.

28

The next morning, Monsieur Tuvache no longer has the strength to get up. His wife tells him not to worry. 'Stay in bed. With the children's help, we'll manage very well. The doctor I've called says that you're having a real nervous breakdown and that you have to rest. I've made an arrangement with Alan's school. He'll miss a few days but it doesn't matter. You know how full of ideas that little chap is.'

'What ideas?'

Mishima attempts to get up: 'I have to mould breeze-blocks, weave ropes, sharpen blades . . .'

But his head is spinning and his wife orders: 'Get back into bed! And don't think about it any more. We'll work out how to run the shop without you.'

And off she goes, leaving the door open so that her husband can call. From downstairs in the shop, Monsieur Tuvache hears imagination preparing for an orgy of activity in the bright light of day. Lucrèce and Marilyn come up the stairs.

'There, my dear, take the basket and go and buy

three legs of lamb, some oranges and bananas . . . and some sugar too! I'm going to prepare it in the old way, and I'll follow Alan's advice as well. It doesn't matter if the lambs didn't commit suicide. It doesn't change the taste. Ernest, would you help me to get rid of all this? So, Vincent, will the first ones be ready soon?'

Mishima detects an odd smell in the air. 'What are you making?'

His wife arrives with a plate, enters the bedroom and answers: 'Crêpes.'

'You mean . . . mourning crêpe?'

'Of course not; don't be silly! The sort of crêpes you eat, of course. Look, Vincent pours batter into the frying pan with the ladle. He designs them in the shape of a skull and leaves holes for the eyeballs, the nasal cavities and the spaces between the teeth. And then, see? He pours in the batter crosswise, in the form of two crossed bones, like on pirate flags.'

'Do you serve them dusted with cyanide?'

'Oh, very funny! I think you need to rest now,' says Lucrèce, leaving the room.

They all bustle about, passing each other in the corridor, like butterflies scattering madness at a whirling ball. At lunchtime, orders are shouted out: 'Two portions of lamb – Lucrèce! Three crêpes – Vincent! Marilyn, would you please go and shake the hand of the gentleman downstairs? Crêpes: two with chocolate and one with sugar.'

'Lucrèce!'

'What now?'

Madame Tuvache enters the bedroom again, wiping her hands on an apron. Her husband, who is horribly tense, asks her: 'What is this place turning into? A restaurant?'

'No, you silly thing, because we're going to have music too!'

'Music?! What kind of music?'

'Alan has some friends who play ancient instruments. I think they're called ... guitars. And besides, that boy's remarkable, you know. He cheers up the victims.'

'What victims?'

'The customers.'

'You call our customers victims? But, Lucrèce ...'

'Oh, everything's fine. I don't have time to argue.'

She goes out again leaving him to a melancholy waltz and vertigo; Mishima seems to be looking though a haze of vapour. Sitting in his bed, wearing a kimono jacket with a red X under the solar plexus, he looks like some oriental thinker ... Chaos churns in his mind and heavy mists swim before his eyes.

Alan passes the room and stops. 'How's it going, Dad?'

What large eyes the child has, this friendly healer of human anxieties. His adored schemes in which unknown treasures sparkle. And his fireworks, his outbursts of joy, which bring laughter to the dumb, shadowy skies of the City of Forgotten Religions.

Something escapes from Mishima's throat like a song that has lost its way. The child goes away.

Monsieur Tuvache would like to get up but he gets tangled in the sheets like a fish struggling in the mesh of the net. He can't manage it, and drops his arms onto the bedcovers.

He can feel the metamorphosis, attributes it entirely to Alan. He knows that now everything at the Suicide Shop has been altered by the skilled little alchemist.

29

'The door!'

Mishima has ordered that the bedroom door be kept shut. In bed, he switches on his TV (3D – with integral sensations) in time for the evening news. He presses one of the many buttons on a remote control.

A female presenter materialises in the room. At first as translucent as a veil, she becomes progressively clearer.

'Good evening. Here is the news.'

She announces nothing but ultra-pessimistic shit. At least there's one person who doesn't disappoint Mishima.

She looks real; seated there on a chair with her arms folded, you would think she was actually in the room. By leaning to right or left, you can see her in profile. Mishima can smell her perfume, which he finds too heady. He diminishes its intensity with the use of his remote control.

The presenter crosses her long, attractive legs. Monsieur Tuvache is not so keen on the colour of her skirt. He swaps its colours round by pressing on the zapper. He clicks a cursor to bring the chair closer to him. The presenter is now by the pillows, as though she is seated at the bedside of a sick man. If Monsieur Tuvache stretches out his hand he can touch her, feel the fabric of her skirt, which he can push up above her delicate-skinned knees. While she is talking, he could also unbutton her blouse if he wanted, but he's not in the mood for that. He listens to her.

Relaxed, leaning forward and with one elbow on her thigh, she whispers the news to him in the manner of an intimate conversation. Gone is the declamatory, solemn tone of the television of yesteryear. The presenter's low, slightly tired Italian voice is beautiful:

'This morning, in the Siberian province, the dictator of the universe, Madame Indira Tu-Ka-Ta, opened a vast complex of eight hundred thousand chimneys six hundred metres tall, which will – we hope – repair the ozone layer round our planet. But I don't believe it,' the presenter says.

Mishima shares her opinion.

'All the experts think that this decision ought to have been taken as early as the twenty-first century,' she goes on, 'and that it's now much too late. Madame President is, however, convinced . . .'

'Of course,' says Mishima.

'. . . as she declared in her inaugural speech. And now, watch out, it will feel as if we are in the middle of this vast territory dotted with ozone chimneys. It is very cold there. Cover yourselves up.'

Mishima's bed is suddenly right in the middle of Siberia. He feels the icy wind, pulls up the covers, sniffs the damp, frozen peat. And, everywhere, very tall chimneys are blowing ozone into the sky. The smell of this gas pricks his eyes a little. Monsieur Tuvache reaches one hand out of bed and touches the ground. It's a long time since he's felt the texture of grass that, when you stretch it, cuts into your fingers a little. He looks at his hand, which shows no sign of injury.

Suddenly Siberia leaves the bedroom. The presenter reappears on her chair. Blonde Marilyn enters, wearing a rippling Spanish gown. She is even more beautiful than the woman on the TV. Her cemetery warden is with her: 'Good evening, Father.'

Monsieur Tuvache's daughter walks through the light that constitutes the presenter. 'It smells like a perfume factory in here,' she says, sitting down on her father's bed.

He turns off the TV. *Click!*

'Father, look at the beautiful bouquet Ernest gave me. He picked flowers from the tombs while he thought of me. Ah, *l'amour*, as the French would say.'

'*La mort?*'

'*L'a-mour* . . . Oh dear, you're not cured at all! You'd feel much better downstairs in the shop with us. You'd soak up the atmosphere with the garlands and the Chinese lanterns – that would put you back on your feet. Do you want me to bring you a pancake?'

'Only if it's stuffed with poisonous mushrooms . . .'

'Oh, Father, you old devil. Look, I'll leave my bunch of flowers from the cemetery on your bedside table. Don't wait for Mother before you go to sleep, because she'll be coming to bed late. Tonight we're going to live it up in the fresh produce section.'

'Live it up?'

30

Several evenings later Mishima, in tired old slippers and wearing the kimono with the red cross (for self-disembowelment) instead of pyjamas, has regained a little strength and the will to get up and attempt a few first weary steps.

Unshaven, with dark rings round his eyes and with his face all crumpled from the folds in the bedcovers, he drags himself along the corridor as if drunk, reaches the little door that gives access to the tower and stands at the top of the stairs that lead down into the shop. And there on the landing, holding onto the banister, he looks down.

And what does he see?

He just can't believe it. The shop, the beautiful shop that belonged to his parents, grandparents, etc., which has been as sober as a hospital mortuary, clean, tidy . . . look what it has become!

On a long banner stretched from one wall to the other above the display units, a slogan is written: 'KILL YOURSELF WITH OLD AGE!' Mishima recognises Alan's writing.

Underneath, a joyous crowd is debating, laughing, gathering on tiptoe to watch three young men in the fresh produce section, singing, playing a lively tune on the gui . . . guitar.

They're clapping their hands in time, ordering skull-and-crossbones pancakes from Vincent, who is making them on a production line, using an electric hotplate placed on the counter. The smoke rising from the frying pan blurs, softens, renders opaque the light of the neon tubes amongst the fragrance of powdered sugar caramelising, of chocolate which sometimes drips, falls, stains the tiled floor. The batter ladle rises, falls, traces crossed tibias across the pan, and Lucrèce operates the drawer of the till. 'One pancake? Three euro-yens. Thank you, sir.'

On the razorblade stand, where the blades have been cleared away, Marilyn is cramming apples (not the ones from the Alan Turing kits) into a juicer, which she uses to extract the fresh juice straight into glasses: 'One euro-yen, please.'

Ernest is giving a demonstration of seppuku, but the blade of the tanto pressing on his belly twists, loops and bends into a figure of eight. Mishima rubs his eyes, and walks down the stairs. The cemetery warden sells three sabres to beaming customers, rolls them up and puts them into bags bearing the word: 'YIPPEE!' Monsieur Tuvache has to duck down to get underneath the garlands, and bumps his head on some festively coloured Chinese lanterns. He tells himself that perhaps he is dreaming. But no, for his wife is calling to him.

'Oh, darling, here you are at last! Well, so much the better. You can help us, because we're worked off our feet. Do you want a pancake?'

A genuinely desperate individual – one who is not aware of the changes at the shop – enters and naturally heads for Mishima, who is wearing the same overwhelmed expression as he is. 'I would like a breeze-block so I can sink to the bottom of the river.'

'A breeze-block . . . Ah! Quite. I'm glad to see someone normal at last. Have they moved them? No, they're still here.'

Monsieur Tuvache takes a deep breath and bends down to hoist one up with both hands, but he's astonished at being able to lift it so easily. The block of mortar seems extraordinarily light to him. He could balance it on one fingertip and spin it round. The few days' rest couldn't have given him so much strength. He examines its texture, scratching it with his nails:

'Polystyrene . . .'

The customer also weighs the breeze-block in his hand.

'But this floats! How am I supposed to drown with it?'

Mishima frowns, raises his eyebrows and shakes his head. 'I suppose it's no good holding onto it with your hands ... but, if the chain is fixed to an ankle, you must be able to drown under the polystyrene breeze-block floating on the surface.'

'What's the point of selling that?'

'To be honest ... I don't know. Do you want a pancake?'

The disconcerted customer looks at the gaudy masked crowd hooting party blowers and dancing idiotically to the loud music.

'Don't these people ever watch the news on TV? Don't they ever despair for the future of the Earth?'

'That's what I was wondering,' replies Mishima to the man who was hoping to spend his night at the bottom of the river. 'I'd willingly accompany you too.'

Overwhelmed, they fall into each other's arms with a wail, and blubber on each other's shoulders while in the fresh produce section Alan, who has hung up a sheet, presents a puppet show in which everything is wonderful, beautiful, unrealistic and inevitably stupid. Vincent looks at home in this country-fair atmosphere with its smoke. With his bandaged cranium he's not smiling, of course, but he does look better.

Lucrèce, who discovers her husband in floods of tears, rushes forward and blames the customer who is holding him in his arms. 'Leave him alone! What have you said to him to get him into this state? Go on, get out!'

'I only wanted to find something to kill myself with tonight,' the other man defends himself.

'Didn't you see the banner above the shelves? Here we don't kill ourselves any more, except with old age! Go on, bugger off.'

And, moving through the happy crowd, she walks back to the staircase with her faltering husband, who asks: 'What are the new tanto blades made of?'

'Rubber.'

'And why did you change the materials for the breeze-blocks?'

'Because when the customers dance, if they bump into the central gondola, I was worried that one of the blocks would fall on their feet. Can you imagine the damage? It's like with the ropes; now we sell the same ones as for bungee jumps. It was Vincent's idea; he says that when people jump off the stool and then hit their heads three or four times on the ceiling, they won't want to do it again. Did you know that we've changed suppliers? No more Don't Give A Damn About Death. Now, we buy everything from Laugh Out Loud. And, since we changed, our turnover has tripled.'

Mishima's knees give way. His wife catches him under the armpits.

'Go on, off to bed, my gloomy one!'

31

Later, when the shop has emptied of customers and the silence of night has descended once more, Madame Tuvache is in Alan's room. Seated on a chair, she watches him sleep. With hands joined and flat on the top of her head, elbows triangling above her shoulders, the arrangement of Lucrèce's arms traces in the air the outline of a great eye on top of a body. The pupil – Madame Tuvache's head, leaning over to one shoulder – seems to be turned and lowered towards Alan's face, which is as delicate as if it were entirely surrounded by gauze and whose every feature speaks of the joy of living.

One day will he have to be put in irons and thrown into the sea, this inventor of brave new worlds? His little snub nose in the air, he dreams of shining paradises. He is an oasis in a desert of boredom. His neck in the hollow of a synthetic pillow, he moves his lips a little, caught in one of the stories of his dreams. His eyelids, as soft as the moon, are closed, rimmed with long lashes, and everything about him engenders a kind of hope that is so anachronistic in this era.

The boy who by day makes human minds dream, asleep looks as innocent as a babbling brook, spilling its happy insouciance over everything. He resembles those beautiful horizons that lead you to unknown places. And his feet under the covers seem ready to run an adventurous race. The smell of his room ... Few perfumes are as fresh as the scent of childhood. He is dreaming up his singular miraculous schemes. Oh, the mind of a child, where fairy tales are constructed!

Tonight, the moon is dreaming more lazily. Madame Tuvache stands up, and caresses Alan's blond curls. He opens his eyes and smiles at her. Then he turns over and goes back to sleep. Life, at his side, seems to be played on a violin.

32

Lucrèce is in bed, beside her husband. Lying on her back with her arms at her sides, an eternal silence hovers above her. The shapes have faded and are no more than a dream now, but then the horrible cloud of her past rises up again, making her slowly bend her knees within herself.

When she was a little girl – four or five years old – her mother would ask her to wait for her after school, sitting on a bench in the playground of the infant school, and promised her that if she was very good, she could have a go on the swings.

Her mother was often late, and sometimes didn't come, so the headmistress of the school would tell the child to go home on her own. Her father, despite his promises, never came. And often in the evening the little girl waited, behaving well, so well; waiting for her mother and the go on the swings.

Did she ever have a go on the swings? Lucrèce doesn't remember. All she can remember is the wait, the wait for her mother who, she imagined, would watch her on the swings.

With her chubby little hands, with the turned-up tips of the fingers, laid flat on her thighs and sitting up tall, not slumping at all, her eyes wide open, she looked straight in front of her. She looked straight in front of her but she saw nothing! She was nothing but good, the very image of goodness, so good that her mother must come!

She forbade herself any movement, any word, any breath of a sigh. She waited so perfectly that her mother could not but come. If the tip of her nose was itching or one little sock had slipped down over her ankle, she remained motionless. Mummy would come. She dissolved into herself, breathed in the itch at the tip of her nose, the cool patch on her calf where her sock had slipped down. She had learned how to absorb that. She knew how to gather herself together, was learning how to become Zen. When, later on, she watches documentaries on ancient Buddhists she will realise that already, at the age of four, she knew how to attain the same mental state. From her childhood, she has retained this ability to absent herself, this way of suddenly seeming to look very far in front of her. There is a great space in her head, just as when she waited for her mother on a bench in the school playground. She was turning to stone there, could no longer feel her body, could swear that she was no longer breathing. When the mother arrived, her daughter would no longer be alive.

Outside, it is raining sulphuric acid on the bedroom windows.

33

'I know, I know perfectly well, I know exactly! What do you think? Everything has changed here while I was depressed; I don't recognise anything any more. It's not the same shop any more – a cow wouldn't be able to find her calf here!'

Mishima has vaguely recovered. He's wearing a waistcoat and checked shirt, while on his head there is a white cardboard cone, decorated with multicoloured circles. A piece of elastic stretches beneath his chin, holding on this hat, which is being observed doubtfully by the very serious man to whom he's speaking and explaining. 'And yet I had ideas for it to continue as it was before. I'd planned to organise an aeroplane cruise around the world. Nobody would have returned from it! We would have offered a selection of the most dangerous regional airlines in the world and the least reliable pilots. At Don't Give A Damn About Death, they had taken on about twenty of them – depressive alcoholics on tranquillisers and always with powder up their noses, even at the controls. We made sure all the luck was on our side. At each stop, the suicidal passengers would board a new dilapidated plane, wondering if it was going to crash into a mountain, at the bottom of an ocean, in a desert, on a town . . . The people wouldn't have known in what part of the globe they were going to die. Yes, but there you go; we've changed our supplier.'

'You shouldn't complain,' comments the man Mishima is talking to, 'because things seem to be going rather well here.' He gazes around him at the large numbers of eager customers entering the Suicide Shop.

The customers kiss Lucrèce affectionately on both cheeks. 'How are you, Madame Tuvache? It's so good to come back to your shop.'

She, disguised as a phial of poison, with a headdress in the form of a cork, offers them the large dishes containing the culinary specialities of the day – Monday: suicidal lamb, beef stifled in steam, duck in blood – which she has noted down on the slate where she used to write the name of the day's poisoned cocktail.

She has had the double central display unit dismantled and taken down to the cellar to make way for a long table where the customers meet to think up solutions for the future of the world.

'To resolve the advance of the desert,' suggests one, 'you'd have to be able to transform the sand into a raw material useful to people, such as has already been done with the forests. Coal, petroleum, gas –'

'Without a doubt, by compacting it and heating it to extreme temperatures,' cuts in another, 'we could turn it into incredibly hard vitrified bricks, which would be vital to construction.'

'Oh yes!' exclaims a girl. 'And so each apartment, bridge or anything else that was built would be a small victory over the dunes.'

'The regions of the world that suffer the most from this calamity would become the wealthiest. That would be great.'

'I shall note down that idea,' enthuses Alan, sitting at the end of the table in an Aladdin costume. 'There's always a solution to everything. We must never despair.'

Hearing those words in his shop does something to Mishima . . .

More and more people love to come here to meet, and to hope, in the Suicide Shop, which they now call TSS, like they might say YMCA.

Dumbfounded, Mishima prefers to stick to the shop's original ethos when facing the stern man in front of him. 'I wanted to install a letter box where customers could slip in a message explaining what they'd done. It's a good idea, don't you think? The relatives of the suicidal person, and friends if there were any, could have come to consult the letters which the dead person had written to them. I tell myself that doubtless afterwards, in their pain, as they explored the shelves they might perhaps have bought something for themselves. I'd planned for several weeks of promotion: hemp week, etc. And two for the price of one on Valentine's Day.'

Marilyn, disguised as the sexy and amusing fairy Carabosse in the fresh produce section, now only touches the customers with her magic wand: 'Zap, you're dead!' A small green light switches on and crackles as it throws out sparks from the tip of the wand as soon as it makes contact. The pretend suicides roll about on the floor, miming horrible convulsions, much to the dismay of Mishima, who despite everything banks the twelve euro-yens for the Death Ki— for any old kiss!

The shopkeeper pulls the elastic from under his chin, as it is pinching the skin of his neck. 'Can you see my daughter's pregnant? By the cemetery warden. She wants to give life.'

The man replies: 'You had three children yourself, so you must have felt some attachment to life.'

'Three children ... The third ...' Mishima puts things into perspective. 'I had planned to implement an idea my eldest had before he was corrupted by the youngest: a simple metal crown placed on the head. At the back there was a small articulated arm, at the end of which a magnifying glass was fixed. And so, in summer, people could commit suicide by sunstroke. All you'd have to do would be to sit in a place with no shade and adjust the magnifying glass until you found the burning point. When your hair started to singe, you'd just have to remain motionless. The concentrated point of the ray would burn the scalp, then the skull. In collecting up the desperate people, wisps of smoke would have been rising from the big, black holes in their burnt skulls . . . But that's no longer on the cards, alas. Look at that one – my eldest – in whom I invested so much pride, see what he's become! A former anorexic with the real psychopathic temperament of a mass killer, he has discovered a new passion for – guess what! – pancakes! Frankly . . . He stuffs himself with them from morn till night.'

Vincent, with very rounded cheeks and short red beard, eyes still furious beneath the head bandage, is dressed up as Death in a clinging black one-piece painted with white bones. Tossing soft pasta in a large salad bowl, he looks at his father, who comes over and pats his son's prominent abdomen. 'The skeleton's putting on a bit of padding, eh!'

Then Mishima turns to the visitor once again

and says: 'As you can see, I had no lack of ideas. At one point it even made me feel a bit off-colour – and that's as long as it took the rest of the family to accomplish their treachery under the influence of the other eternally delighted one, the Optimist over there . . . And now see what's happened. Look at this: our new disposable pistols fire blanks, and the only harm the Sweets of Death do is to teeth. As for the ropes for people to hang themselves, if I were to tell you . . . And the sabres for seppuku serve as fly-swatters.'

'Yes, but . . . what about our bit of business?' asks the visitor anxiously. He has the look of an official person who has been sent here on a special mission. 'It involves the collective suicide of all the members of the regional government! We can hardly give them fly-swatters.'

'What would you have liked?'

'I'm not really sure . . . I've heard about that poison – Sandman? – if you have enough left in stock for forty people.'

Mishima calls to his wife, disguised as a twisted phial of poison, who is standing by the meeting table, listening to all the 'we could haves', 'we'd only have had tos', 'we're going to do this and thats', etc . . .

'Lucrèce! Have you still got some belladonna, deadly gel and desert breath in the scullery?'

'What for?'

'What for . . .' sighs the shopkeeper, facing the government envoy. 'I can assure you there are times when she loses the plot, that one . . .'

Then he raises his voice and addresses his wife again: 'The government, recognising its own incompetence and its culpability, has decided to commit mass suicide tonight, live on TV! Can you prepare what's needed?'

'I'll go and see what I have! Will you help me, Alan?'

'Yes, Mother.'

34

'Who did this? Who dared? Who's the bastard . . . ?'

Mishima emerges from the apartment, his eyes spinning like flying saucers. He finishes tying the (yellow) belt of a kimono jacket bearing a red cross on the solar plexus.

Legs apart and arms outspread, he is now gripping a tanto with a sharpened, gleaming blade (not a rubber one), which he took down from above the sideboard in the dining room.

He swallows a small glass of sake in a single gulp. At the top of the steps and with flowered slippers on his feet, he is every bit as menacing as a samurai about to attack. He even sounds as if he's speaking Japanese: 'Hoo di dit? Hoo?'

He asks who did it, but instinctively descends towards Alan, who is innocently manipulating some marionettes in the fresh produce section.

Lucrèce, hands flat on her head, swiftly lowers them and steps in front of her husband. 'What's going on now, darling?'

She seems to be gazing far into the distance while her husband cleaves the air with sweeping strokes of his blade, attempting to reach Alan, who ducks away, slips between his father's legs and climbs the stairs.

'Grrr!'

Monsieur Tuvache turns round and pursues him. At the top of the steps Alan, rather than find himself trapped in his bedroom or one of the other rooms in the apartment, chooses to open the little door on the left – the one that gives access to the spiral staircase in the tower. His father pursues him up the slippery steps of worn stone. The blade of his sabre strikes sparks as it touches the walls while he roars: 'Who is the bastard who put laughing gas into the government's cocktail?'

Madame Tuvache, thinking that her husband is going to kill her little one, returns from the scullery with a bottle of belladonna and also rushes up the tower's narrow staircase, only to be followed shortly afterwards by Marilyn, who cries 'Mother!', and then Vincent. Ernest – still a little lost in the cloud of sulphuric acid – asks, 'What's going on?'

'Going on? Going on!'

Monsieur Tuvache, also breathless after climbing the stairs, chokes as he is joined on the platform of the tall, narrow tower by the rest of his family. The paved area is circular and covered by a conical slate roof with an exposed timber frame. In the walls, slits are open to the sky, like the arrow-slits in battlements, no doubt so that the sound of the bells could travel further in the old days, or the voice or loudspeaker belonging to some long-deceased muezzin. Here, a breeze makes a continuous wailing sound. Marilyn's flared and pleated white dress flies up as she thrusts her arms and wrists between her thighs to hold it down. It is night-time. Red and green neon signs displaying gigantic Chinese advertisements light up the tower. Madame Tuvache picks up the bottle filled with liquid belladonna, raises it to her lips and threatens her husband as he approaches Alan:

'If you kill him, I'll kill myself!'

'So will I!' says Marilyn, buckling up the chin-strap of the helmet containing two sticks of dynamite, which Vincent gave her for her coming of age. In her hands she grips the wires of the detonators.

The eldest Tuvache child has pressed the cutting edge of a thick-bladed kitchen knife to his own throat: 'Go on, Dad . . .'

Mishima blurts: 'It's not him I want to kill, it's me!'

The neck of the bottle is right up against Lucrèce's lips, and she won't back down. 'If you kill yourself, I'll kill myself!'

'Meeh oo . . .' says Marilyn's muffled voice

inside the helmet with the armour-plated visor, meaning 'Me too.'

'Go on, Dad,' repeats Vincent's crazy voice as he stuffs down a pancake.

'So will this never end?' cuts in the gentle Ernest, suddenly beside himself with anger. 'Marilyn, darling, you're going to be a mother! And what about you, Father? If you do this, who'll run the shop?'

'There is no Suicide Shop any more!' declares Mishima.

This puts a damper on proceedings.

'What do you mean?' asks Lucrèce, suddenly lowering the bottle of belladonna.

'They're going to destroy the shop! At best, they'll close it tomorrow morning.'

'Uh oo? (But who?),' Marilyn wants to know.

'Those we made fools of tonight.'

The wind gusts around the top of the tower, whistles over the edges of the walls. Alan steps back as his father comes forward and explains:

'After the head of the government made his speech criticising himself, live on the televised bulletin, he took the stopper from a phial of Sandman in front of him and inhaled it. All the regional ministers and secretaries of state did the same. None of them touched the cocktail or swallowed it (that was a worthwhile precaution!).

But they all burst out in an enormous attack of laughter, each one in turn describing a childhood terror while laughing uproariously. The finance minister said: "When I went on holiday to my grandmother's house in the country, she woke me every morning by throwing live adders into my bed. Well, actually they were dead grass snakes, but boy was I scared! When I came back to the City of Forgotten Religions, I stammered with terror and peed in my pants. Uh-oh! Now it's starting again . . ." And there was indeed a smell of urine in the room. The minister of defence intervened: "I was told: close your eyes and open your mouth. I thought it was to give me some sweets but I was made to swallow rabbit droppings! Argh . . .!" And he started rolling about on the floor, and hopping around as if he was a little rabbit. "I remember when I was eleven," said the minister for the environment, "I was forbidden to pick flowers from the hedges. I was told they were thunder-flowers and that if I picked one, a thunderbolt would fall on me. Well, I tell you, that was back in the days when there were still flowers on the banks! Ha, ha, ha! Now that I've become a minister, there's no risk of it happening again, oh, ha, ha! There aren't any wild flowers any more!" Then he tore out his hair in handfuls, laughing: "He loves me, he loves me not!" I was dumbfounded, no doubt like all the TV viewers and I had to flick off some of the minister's hair, which had fallen onto my sleeves. "As for me, one time ..." at last declaimed the president, who was weeping with laughter, "an uncle imprisoned me in a potato sack, which he placed on the flat back of a cart and then whipped his horse to make him set off at a gallop. Thrown around in the chaos on the cart, I fell off, and found myself at the side of the road, still imprisoned in a potato sack! Aaah! They should have left me there. Oh! I wouldn't have led my region to disaster. Oh! Oh, oh, oh!" This was a crazy televised bulletin, which the producer had to stop suddenly because the cameramen in the studio were so doubled up with laughter too. The zigzags of their 3D-integral-sensations camera were bouncing around in all directions. You couldn't see or understand anything any more. All of this because a scoundrel ... made the members of the government breathe in laughing gas! Well, Alan?' Finally he rolls his eyes, in which Chinese advertisements are reflected.

The eleven-year-old child recoils. 'But, Father, I didn't know! I was wearing Mother's gas mask and I didn't notice. I took the bottle of desert breath from its usual place, but I'd forgotten we'd changed suppliers ... and now it's Laugh Out Loud who delivers to us ...'

His father advances, arm stretched out and holding the hilt of his tanto, the point of its blade pricking the red silk cross on his kimono jacket. His head, dripping with sweat, gleams with sliding colours. His wife walks at his side, ready to swallow a litre and a half of belladonna. Marilyn, with the big black helmet enclosing her head, looks like a fly from a nightmare. In her ultra-sexy dress, the kind worn by a film actress, she advances blindly, gripping two detonators in her fists. As for Vincent the artist, illuminated like a ridiculous fakir, grimacing horribly and belching after a pancake, he's savouring in advance the squirt of red paint that will shoot out of the tube in his throat.

Alan backs away in panic from the incomprehensible sight of his whole family caught up in the storm about to break and turn people into corpses, right in front of him! An advertisement for effervescent tablets sends its three-storey bubbles climbing up the entire height of the Zeus tower.

Alan rejects the inevitable and stretches out a hand. 'No, no! Don't do this ...' He draws back and stumbles.

He disappears backwards through one of the

openings. His legs shoot into the air and drop straight down. Lucrèce, Mishima, Marilyn, Vincent, and Ernest too, abandon everything on the flagstones – the bottle of belladonna, the tanto, the knife – to rush forward and bend over the opening. Marilyn, who's getting tangled up in the detonator wires of the integral helmet with the visor that blinds her, asks: 'What's happened?'

Her cemetery warden unfastens the strap and replies: 'Alan has fallen through the window.'

'*What?*'

'But he's not yet squashed on Boulevard Bérégovoy!'

Alan is there, a storey below at the edge of a small roof, suspended by his right hand from a zinc gutter whose rivets are giving way and popping out, one by one. It looks like his left shoulder was hurt in the fall so he can't move his arm. The gutter is splitting and bending over, taking Alan with it. It is about to break completely. It's then that a long, white ribbon descends, on its way to reach the child. Vincent is unwinding his turban! Fast as lightning and bending over the void, he unrolls the immensely long crêpe bandage from his head, and it soon reaches Alan's right hand. He seizes it just as the gutter comes off and falls away, bouncing off the pavement down below in the depths of the darkness. His flabbergasted parents and sister turn towards Alan's elder brother, whose clenched fists are still gripping the long bandage at the end of which Alan is dangling.

'Quick, help me!'

Mishima, Lucrèce, Marilyn and Ernest leap to Vincent's aid and together they pull gently on the bandage to prevent it tearing. Alan comes up, in a series of small jolts. With ten careful hands, they bring him back towards them. They are almost there. As the child, who is light, rises, they let down the crêpe bandage they've pulled in, in order to double or triple its thickness and safety.

'I was so afraid,' confesses Lucrèce.

'It's a good job you were here, my lad,' sighs Mishima.

'My head doesn't hurt any more!' exclaims Vincent in astonishment.

'Our boy shall be called Alan,' decides Marilyn, with tears in her eyes. 'If it's a girl, she'll be Alanne.'

Ernest nods his agreement and the little Tuvache boy climbs, climbs. Hanging in the air, he observes the heads bent towards him, the faces of his father, his mother, sister, brother and almost brother-in-law.

Mishima laughs. 'In any case, we wouldn't have to worry if the regional government did close the

Suicide Shop by decree! With the money we've earned recently by selling jokes and novelties, we've got enough to move to the other side of the boulevard and take over management of the François Vatel, which we'd rename Better Than the Shop Opposite. We'd turn it into –'

'A crêperie?' asks Vincent.

'If you like!' laughs Monsieur Tuvache. Since his birth, his youngest child has never seen him as joyful as he is here.

The eldest child is radiant too (which is new) as he pulls on the bandage:

'I'll stop doing the skulls – it's getting a bit tiresome – to make pancakes as round as Alan's face, with two holes for his laughing eyes and a slit for his big optimistic smile. Around the pancake, with batter drizzled from the ladle, I'll trace golden curls and I'll dust the cheeks with a little chocolate powder for his freckles. Even people with no appetite would want to hang that up under glass above their beds so they could believe in something nice.'

'*Oh, oh, that would be happiness ...!*' sings Lucrèce. Her youngest child has never heard her sing before.

And the child rises up, holding on with one hand. He's no more than three metres from them. Chinese ideograms slide over the back of his bright pullover and trousers. Gripping the bandage, without calling for help, and without fear or bitterness for what they have been, Alan looks at them as he rises upwards, jolt by jolt. Their collective happiness, their sudden faith in the future and those radiant smiles on their faces are his life's work. Two metres away from him, his sister is laughing. Madame Tuvache watches him approaching as if she has suddenly seen her mother arrive in the school playground. Alan's mission is accomplished.

He lets go.